Whatever After

ABBY IN OZ

Read all the Whatever After books!

SPECIAL EDITION #2

Whatever After

ABBY IN OZ

SARAH MLYNOWSKI

Scholastic Inc.

This book was originally published in hardcover by Scholastic Press in 2020.

All rights reserved. Published by Scholastic Inc., *Publishers since 1920.* SCHOLASTIC and associated logos are trademarks and/or registered trademarks of Scholastic Inc.

The publisher does not have any control over and does not assume any responsibility for author or third-party websites or their content.

ISBN 978-0-545-74673-1

10 9 8 7 6 5 4 3 2   22 23 24 25

Printed in the U.S.A.   40

This edition first printing 2021

for my mom, elissa harris ambrose,
because she made me believe in magic,
and watched the wizard of oz with me
at least a hundred times

chapter one

There Are No Tornadoes in Smithville

*t*he sun is shining and it's a beautiful spring afternoon, but I am not feeling my one hundred percent best. I think I'm getting a cold. My nose is all stuffed up. Also, I'm standing on a rickety ladder outside a tree house, holding my dog, Prince, in my arms, which is not the most comfortable position. Sure, Prince is adorable, but he's starting to get heavy.

I knock on the tree house door. "Robin? Frankie? Penny?" I call. "Are you guys in there?"

The tree house is in my friend Robin's backyard. Robin's

parents built it for her a few years ago. It has a roof and a door and a window like a real little house, and it's always fun to hang out in.

Not so long ago, I got to visit another tree house inside the fairy tale of *Little Red Riding Hood*. But I'll explain that later.

"Coming!" Robin calls, and I hear her footsteps inside.

Frankie, Robin, me (Abby), and Penny — otherwise known as FRAP — are getting together today to work on our group project for school. I have a great idea for it. It involves dogs.

Robin and Frankie are my two best friends. Penny is my sometimes friend. Meaning sometimes I want to hang out with her, sometimes I wish she'd transfer to another school.

We had a half day today, so Penny and Frankie came straight to Robin's after school. But Robin asked me if I could go home first and get Prince, which I did. Robin wants a dog of her own, but her parents say she should spend some time with actual dogs before they get one.

"Abby!" Robin cries, flinging open the tree house door

with a grin. She just got braces, which make her look like a teenager. Her reddish hair is up in a loose bun, with a few curls framing her freckled face. "Yay, you really brought Prince. You have the *cutest* dog." She takes him from my arms as I bend my way through the door. "You look like a teddy bear," Robin coos to Prince, "yes you do."

Prince barks happily, as if to say *Thank you*.

Penny scowls from her perch on a cushion on the floor. "I don't see why you want a dog," she tells Robin, flicking her long blonde ponytail over her shoulder. "You have to take them for walks even when it rains. And they drool. And they're messy. And they smell."

Hello to you, too, Penny. "They don't smell," I say, sitting down on the cushion next to Frankie, who is curled up on her own cushion.

"They *sometimes* smell," Frankie says.

I look at her in surprise. Frankie is supposed to be on *my* side.

"Well, sometimes," I admit. "But not if you give them regular baths. Prince doesn't smell." At least not today.

"Wanting a horse, I understand," Penny says. "I love horses. But a dog? No thanks."

"Abby," Robin says, plopping down on the cushion next to Penny, "where did you get Prince? An animal shelter or a breeder?"

Nope and nope. "We got him as a present," I say. Which is kind of true. But Robin would never believe the real truth.

I got Prince when my brother and I went into a fairy tale.

I know it sounds totally bonkers, but there's a magic mirror in the basement of my house. And a fairy, Maryrose, is trapped inside it. She takes me and my younger brother, Jonah, through the mirror into different fairy tales. Like *Little Red Riding Hood. Cinderella. Beauty and the Beast.* I think one day she's planning to bring us into the story that trapped her so that we can help set her free.

Anyway, when Jonah and I fell into the story of *Sleeping Beauty*, we got Prince as a gift. And then we took him home with us, because he is adorable.

Of course, we had to make up a whole story for our

parents because they don't know about Maryrose, the mirror, or the whole traveling-to-fairy-tales thing. My nana does, though. She actually went into *Little Red Riding Hood* with us.

Guess who else knows about my magic mirror?

You're not going to believe it.

It's very unfortunate.

It's . . . Penny.

Yeah. Penny.

Penny, my sometimes friend, knows about Maryrose and the fairy tales and everything.

Why?

Because one time, Frankie, Robin, Penny, and I all fell into the story of *Alice's Adventures in Wonderland*. Maryrose had nothing to do with taking us into *Alice*. That was all Gluck. Gluck is an evil fairy who's trying to stop me from freeing Maryrose. He lured me and my friends into the book, and we almost got trapped there forever. Luckily, we escaped. As we were leaving the story, Frankie and Robin got sprinkled with a magical powder that made them lose their memories of the

5

ence. But Penny and I did *not* get sprinkled.

Which means that, ever since then, Penny keeps asking if she can sleep over at my house so she can go into a fairy tale with me. But I don't think that's the best idea. Fairy tales can be dangerous. Penny would never listen to me if we went into one, and who knows how she would mess the story up. Never mind that every time she and I are with Frankie and Robin, I worry Penny's going to blow my secret.

"Can we get started on our project?" Frankie asks, snapping me back to reality. She adjusts her red-framed glasses and pushes her dark-brown hair out of her eyes. "We don't have all day."

Whoa. What is up with Frankie? Sure, she likes to get good grades in school, but she's never testy like this. I hope everything's okay. I'm about to ask her what's going on when my nose itches and I sneeze.

Achoo!

"Bless you," Robin and Frankie say at the same time.

"Ew, are you sick?" Penny asks, scooting away from me. "You better not get me sick."

"I'm not sick," I say quickly. No one wants to be around a sick person. And I really don't want to be a sick person. If I pretend I'm not getting sick, maybe my body will believe it? "I'm just a little . . . stuffed up. It might be allergies." I do sometimes get sneezy in the springtime. I glance out the window. It's strange . . . but the sky is not as blue as it was just a few minutes ago. And the sun seems to have disappeared. Dark gray clouds are gathering, and the wind is picking up.

"Abby, you're not allergic to Prince, are you?" Robin asks. She lets go of Prince, who trots into the middle of the tree house and curls up on the purple shag rug to take a snooze. Prince can nap anywhere.

Frankie groans. "Robin! Of course Abby isn't allergic to her *own* dog. Then she'd be sneezing every day, not just today."

Robin blushes, and I frown. Frankie might be right but she doesn't have to be mean about it.

"Listen," Penny pipes up. "I have the *best* idea for our project."

"I have a great idea, too," I add quickly, just in case Penny thinks she's in charge of this thing.

Our assignment is to start our own small business — one that will help the community. The project is due in two weeks, so today we are supposed to settle on an idea.

"I'll start," says Penny. She puts a piece of grape bubble gum in her mouth without offering us any, and then pulls a new red notebook and sparkly pen out of her backpack.

I wish I had brought a sparkly pen. And a new red notebook. And bubble gum.

Penny turns the notebook to the first page and begins reading from a paragraph she clearly wrote earlier. "Our new business will help the community by teaching kids in our class to up their style game. For a small fee, we'll give them new hairstyle suggestions, or tell them that the headband they're wearing makes them look like they're seven."

My mouth drops open. "You want us to give the kids in our class hair advice?"

Penny blows a big bubble with her gum, then sucks it back

in. "Not *just* hair advice. Clothing advice, too. Everyone needs help with how they look. For example, Abby, did you know your T-shirt has a stain on it?"

Wait, what?

"No, it doesn't!" Frankie protests.

"Yes, it does. Frankie, maybe your glasses aren't strong enough. But look on her right side, near her armpit." Penny points at my armpit. "Under the blue stripe. There's a little blue dot. A pen dot perhaps. Not sure how that got there, or why, but it's obviously not supposed to be on your shirt."

I look down my armpit. At first I don't see anything, but then I do. A teeny tiny blue dot. How did Penny even see that? It's the size of a piece of dust. "No one's going to notice that," I say.

Penny smirks. "I noticed it. If I can see, so will other people. So unless you can get that stain out in the wash, which I bet you can't, you need to retire the shirt. Stripes are out this season anyway."

But I love this shirt!

"Penny," Frankie says. "I don't think being critical of people counts as helping the community."

"I agree," Robin adds.

"Thanks," I tell my friends.

"But my being critical will *help* people," Penny says. "I have an eye for fashion. Have you seen my new shoes? Aren't they cute?"

Her new shoes *are* cute. They're black-and-white-checkered slip-on sneakers. Her whole outfit looks great, actually. She's wearing shiny black jeans and an off-the-shoulder pink top. The top is pen-stain free, obviously.

I'm just wearing jeans and my stained striped T-shirt. Robin is wearing a cute blue dress and a green hoodie, and Frankie is wearing polka-dot leggings and a T-shirt with the NASA logo.

"I still think we should try an idea that doesn't insult anyone," I say. "Like mine."

Penny rolls her eyes. "Fine. Let's hear it."

I sit up straight. "Well," I begin, "a lot of people in Smithville have dogs." I nod at a still sleeping Prince. "My idea is that we start a dog-walking service for people who can't leave their homes for some reason. Maybe they have a sprained ankle. Or are sick." I sneeze again.

"You better not sneeze on me," Penny warns. "And your idea isn't as good as mine. Because not everyone has a dog. I don't. Frankie doesn't. And even Robin doesn't."

"Yet," Robin says.

"Whatever," Penny says. "Our idea should help *everyone*."

"What if we start a tutoring service?" Frankie suggests.

"What would we tutor?" Penny asks.

"Science," Frankie says. "Math. English."

"Boring," Penny says. She smacks her gum. Loudly.

"You could tutor art," Frankie points out.

"True," Penny says, nodding. "I *am* an extremely talented artist. Best in our grade, for sure."

I roll my eyes. Although she's not wrong.

"I don't know," Robin says with a frown. "I need to *be* tutored, not to be a tutor. So I'm not sure that would work."

"Do you have any ideas?" Frankie asks her.

Robin shakes her head. "Not really."

"So what are we going to do?" Frankie asks. "We have to choose something."

"I like my idea," I say.

"Well, I like mine," Penny says.

"And I like mine," Frankie says.

We all look at Robin, but she shrugs, refusing to pick a side.

Sigh. Group projects are the worst.

Achoo! I sneeze again.

"What was that?" Penny asks.

"It was just a sneeze, Penny," I say. "And I covered my nose!"

"Not *that*." She pauses. "That."

I listen hard. And suddenly I *do* hear something.

Whirrr. Whirrrrrr.

"It sounds kind of like a blender," I say.

12

"Maybe my dad is making us smoothies," Robin says.

"I don't think we'd hear the blender all the way out here," Frankie says.

Whirr-whirr! WHIRRRRR!

It's getting louder. And louder. And louder. Now it's like a *roaring* blender.

Prince wakes up with a start and lets out a low growl.

The gray sky outside is getting even darker. It almost looks like nighttime! And the wind is howling.

"Ugh," Penny says. "Is it going to rain? I don't want my new shoes to get ruined!"

Prince suddenly bolts toward the window and starts barking wildly, like five doorbells just went off at the same time.

What is going on?

The blender sound intensifies.

WHIRRRRR! WHIRRRRRRRRRRRR!

"Guys?" Robin says. "This is kind of scary."

I shiver. It totally is! Suddenly, the group project is the last thing on anyone's mind — I can tell.

I push myself off the pillow and follow Prince to the window.

And what I see makes me freeze.

Whoa. Whoa. WHOA.

There is a huge, gray, funnel-shaped spinning thing in the sky! It's the size of a tall building. As it spins, it tilts on its side.

Ahhhh!

"What. Is. That?" Penny shrieks.

"I think it's a tornado," Frankie says in a trembling voice.

That's impossible, right? There are no tornadoes in Smithville!

"Um, guys?" Robin calls over the *WHIRR*ing noise and the sound of Prince's barks. "It's coming straight for us."

I gasp. The spinning funnel shape definitely seems to be moving closer. My heart jumps and I grab Prince. This is bad.

"We need to get out of the tree house!" Penny yells in a panic.

"I don't think there's time," Frankie cries. "We don't want to be outside when it hits!"

OMG. The tornado is now IN Robin's yard. I watch as it sucks up an orange flowerpot like juice with a straw.

I hug Prince tighter and crouch down. "It's about to hit us!" I cry.

We all scream as the tornado crashes right into the tree house.

chapter two

Getting Carried Away

We're inside it! We are *inside* a tornado! OMG! It swallowed us like it did the flowerpot.

I feel the tree house being lifted up and whirled around. It's like we're on a spinning ride at an amusement park. Only, this isn't any fun!

Okay, maybe it's a TEENSY bit fun. But it would be more fun if it weren't so scary.

We're going round and round and round. I hold on to

Prince with one hand, and with my other hand I squeeze the window ledge tightly. My knuckles are white.

Ruff! Ruff! RUFFFFFF! Prince barks, and he slips out of my grasp. Oh, no!

Robin, Penny, and Frankie are still on their cushions on the floor, sliding back and forth. The tree house keeps tilting and whirling and spinning, making me feel dizzy and sick.

Please don't throw up. Please don't throw up.

I cannot think of anything more embarrassing than vomiting all over my friend's tree house.

We all go sliding to the left. Ahhhhhhhhhhhh! I see Prince fly through the air.

We all go sliding to the right. Ahhhhhhhhhhhh! Prince flies through the air in the other direction.

I reach out to try and grab him but I can't. We're moving too fast.

And then we're dropping! We're falling from the sky!

"Hold on tight!" I scream as we —

SMASH.

— land on the ground.

Everything is still.

Everything is quiet.

Somehow, I'm still standing even though every part of my body is shaking. My feet feel like jelly.

The tree house is back on the ground and no longer tilted on one side.

WHEW. We must have plonked back down in another part of Robin's backyard. Any second I'm sure her parents will come running out of the main house to check on us.

Ruff! Ruff! Prince barks, and darts over to me. I pick him up and his little legs are quivering.

"Poor baby," I say, nuzzling his head and ears. "You okay?"

He whimpers and licks my face.

"Is everyone else okay?" I ask, looking up.

Frankie, Robin, and Penny are slowly standing up from the ground. Their eyes are huge and they all look disheveled. Even Penny.

"That. Was. Intense," Penny says. "I think I swallowed my gum!"

"So intense," Robin says. "And really scary."

"*So* scary," Frankie says. "I can't believe the whole tree house got picked up and *moved.*"

"Are we somewhere in my backyard?" Robin asks.

I turn back to the window. Miraculously, it isn't broken, but it's all fogged up. I try to wipe it with my sleeve, but it keeps fogging up again.

"We should get out of here," Frankie says. "In case the tree house is about to collapse in on itself or something."

Eek.

She reaches for the door handle and tries to pull it open, but it doesn't budge.

"It's stuck," Frankie says.

"Let me see," I say. "I think it's just locked."

I unlock it and pull the door open.

The sun is shining. The sky is bright blue. The wind is gone.

And this is for sure not Robin's backyard.

Robin's main house is gone. Instead, there are beautiful, tall flowers all around us. Daffodils and sunflowers and tulips in a million different colors. Red, blue, purple, pink, and the stems go up to our knees! There's a bridge nearby that crosses a bright blue stream. It's like we're in the most beautiful garden ever. And it's all in Technicolor.

All four of us step outside onto the lush grass. I'm still holding Prince in my arms.

"Wow," Robin says. "That tornado took us at least a block away."

Shivers spread down my spine.

Why do I get the feeling that we're much more than a block away? I'm almost positive that, somehow, the tornado took us to a different world, the way my magic mirror does. But where could we be? A fairy tale? A book? Or somewhere else?

Prince squirms out of my arms and I put him down on what looks like a road.

A yellow road. A yellow road made of bricks.

Wait.

A yellow road made of bricks?

A yellow brick road?

A yellow brick road!

A tornado!

Far off on the horizon, I see a massive wall of green. Bright, sparkling green. Emerald colored, even.

An emerald city?

NO. Way.

Oh, wow.

The Emerald City!

It's Oz. It has to be.

We're in *The Wizard of Oz*!

Penny grabs my arm. "Abby," she whispers.

"Yes?" I squeak.

She laughs. "I've got a feeling we're not in Smithville anymore."

I smile. I can't help it. "Have you figured out where we are?"

"I have!" she squeals.

"Me too," I say, laughing.

I love *The Wizard of Oz*! I've never read the book, but I've definitely seen the movie. It's about a girl named Dorothy who gets whisked away by a tornado from her farm in Kansas to the magical Land of Oz.

I sneeze again, but Penny is in too good of a mood to notice. She bends to sniff a hot-pink tulip and does a little dance. "I've been wishing for something like this to happen ever since our last adventure! Hurrah!"

Frankie, still understandably clueless, puts her hands on her hips. "Are you guys going to tell us what's happening or just make us feel bad for not knowing?"

"Oh, you know where we are, too," Penny says. And then she points to the right. "Look over there."

We turn to look.

There are a bunch of short men and women, about my height, dressed in blue, whispering to one another. They are all wearing tall, pointy hats with bells on them. Pointy boots, too. They keep looking at us and looking away.

"Who are they?" Frankie asks.

"They're Munchkins," I say.

"Munchkins?" Robin repeats, looking confused. "The donut holes?"

"Not *that* kind of Munchkin," Penny says. "They're people, not food. Think about it. Munchkins. A yellow brick road. A tornado that carried us away . . . sound familiar?"

Frankie crosses her arms. "Penny, clearly you're referring to *The Wizard of Oz*."

"Like . . . the movie?" Robin asks.

Frankie nods. "A movie based on the book called *The Wonderful Wizard of Oz* by L. Frank Baum. There are fourteen books in the Oz series, but I only read the first one."

"I never read it," Robin says, shrugging. "Or saw the movie."

"Really?" I ask. "How can that be? It's a classic!"

Robin shrugs again. "I don't think it's on Netflix."

"Well, you'll get to see a whole lot of Oz right now!" Penny says excitedly. "Because that's where we are."

"Do you mean like Disneyland?" Frankie asks, looking around. "Or Harry Potter World? Did they make an Oz World?"

Penny beams. "No, I mean we're *in* actual Oz."

Frankie throws her arms in the air. "How is that possible?"

"You might want to ask Abby about that," Penny says, grinning, but then instead of letting me answer she continues. "She has a magic mirror in her basement, and while she refuses to take me through it, sometimes the magic pulls her into different books, which is probably what happened here. We all went to *Alice in Wonderland* together, but you guys don't remember because of the magic powder. But I do. And it was awesome."

Frankie frowns. "Penny? Did you hit your head on the wall during the tornado? I think you might have."

I sigh. I guess I have to tell them the whole story. "She didn't hit her head. The four of us really did go into *Alice's Adventures in Wonderland*. And now it seems like we're really inside *The Wonderful Wizard of Oz*."

24

"Abby," Frankie says, looking worried. "I think you may have hit your head, too."

I guess it's possible, but it's more possible that the same thing that happened when we went into *Alice's Adventures in Wonderland* is happening again.

And that thing is an evil fairy named Gluck.

Did Gluck create the tornado to send us here? To *trap* us here? So I'll stop trying to save Maryrose?

Yeah. He probably did.

And now the four of us are here in a story. Again.

Crumbs.

Woof! Woof-woof! Prince starts barking again and running around in a circle. I freeze. Did Prince just spot Gluck somewhere? I glance around but don't see anyone aside from the Munchkins, who seem to be ignoring us.

Prince peers up at the sky and howls. Uh-oh. I hope it's not another tornado.

I look up, too. We all do. Frankie, Robin, Penny. The Munchkins.

Oh, wow. A house is in the sky!

IN THE SKY. Flying in the sky? No. Falling from the sky!

The house is falling faster and faster — and it's headed right toward us!

Ahhhh!

"Run!" I order.

We all dive for cover. I hide behind a row of sunflowers, cradling Prince in my arms. Frankie, Robin, and Penny crouch down beside us. And the Munchkins seem to vanish from sight entirely.

Then, with an ear-smashing *crack*, the house lands right on top of Robin's tree house. Since the house that fell is an actual-sized house, and made of brick, there is nothing left of the tree house at all. It's just totally gone. Smashed to smithereens.

Poor Robin!

I cough and sneeze, though not from my cold. Dust from the crash is everywhere. I wave the air in front of my face to try and see.

Wait — the door to the house is opening.

The dust begins to clear.

We're all staring at the house's door.

A girl steps out. She's wearing a blue-and-white gingham dress and white chunky shoes, and is holding a small picnic basket. Her brown hair is woven into two braids that fall just past her shoulders. She has pale skin and big brown eyes, and she looks a little younger than me and my friends.

She's also carrying a little black dog.

I gasp. It's . . . *her*. It's Dorothy!

chapter three

Ding-Dong, the Witch Isn't Dead

b elieve us now?" Penny says to Frankie and Robin.

They both just stare at Dorothy, awestruck.

Penny runs over to Dorothy. "Hi, Dorothy. I'm so psyched to meet you! I love your dress. It's so . . . *Wizard of Oz*!"

Dorothy looks at Penny, her big brown eyes getting even bigger. She's clearly freaked out. "How do you know my name?" She glances all around. "Where am I?"

I stand up, still holding Prince, and make my way over to

Dorothy. I need to explain everything to her. Penny hasn't yet learned how to talk to story characters. You have to ease them into things and not give away too much information. You don't want them learning something they shouldn't know, which could lead to them messing up their own story.

Frankie and Robin follow me, still awestruck. But before I can say anything to Dorothy, Prince springs out of my arms and bounds toward her. He leaps up on his hind legs, his tail wagging, and barks excitedly at the little black dog in Dorothy's arms. Oh! Prince never gets to see another dog when we fall into stories! He must be happy to have a new friend.

But Toto whimpers and cowers against Dorothy. He does *not* look happy to see Prince.

"Down, Prince!" I say. "You're scaring Toto!"

Dorothy frowns at me and clutches Toto even closer to her. "How do you know my dog's name? *Where are we?* What's going on? I'm so confused!"

"Join the club," Robin says.

"Listen," I say, turning to Frankie and Robin. "I know it seems impossible, but we really are inside *The Wonderful Wizard of Oz*. And we really have to figure out how to get out of here."

As soon as possible. Gluck could be anywhere. Or anyone. When we were in *Alice's Adventures in Wonderland*, he turned into the White Rabbit to trick us.

"We're really not dreaming?" Frankie asks.

I shake my head. "Do you want me to pinch you?"

She puts out her arm.

I pinch her.

"Ouch. Not dreaming," Frankie says. "And that house falling was no special effect. And this is clearly Dorothy. So . . . I guess we're in Oz?"

"We are definitely in Oz," I say.

Robin blushes. "Since I've never seen the movie, can you guys tell me what the whole story is about?"

"Of course," I say, feeling bad that she's embarrassed. "See, there's a girl named Dorothy."

"Me?" Dorothy squeaks.

"Yes," I say. "And you live with your aunt and uncle in Kansas. Right?"

"This is really creeping me out," Dorothy says, taking a step back.

Oops. So much for easing her into things.

This is why I never tell the story in front of the main character. Knowing your future can cause you to make different decisions. And we don't want to mess up Dorothy's story.

Okay. Change of plans.

"I mean, there's a girl named *Dotty*," I say, looking at my friends meaningfully. "Everyone got it? *Dotty*. Not Dorothy. Good?"

My friends nod, clearly catching my don't-freak-out-Dorothy drift.

"And *Dotty* got caught in a tornado. It picked up her house and took her to the magical Land of Oz. And when the tornado dropped her house, it landed right on the Wicked Witch of the East and, um, killed the witch. And then —"

Wait a sec. Something occurs to me then. Dotty — I mean Dorothy — *didn't* land on the Wicked Witch of the East! She landed on Robin's tree house! And I definitely didn't see the Wicked Witch of the East under the tree house!

Just to be sure, I look over to where Dorothy's house sits. In the movie, there was a pair of witch's legs sticking out from under the house. But now . . . no legs. No witch.

Uh-oh. Did we already mess up the story?

Wait. Maybe what happened in the book is different from what happened in the movie. My mom says movie people sometimes change the original story to make it more Hollywood-y. For instance, in the original *Snow Queen*, there's no Anna or Elsa. And in the original *Little Mermaid*, the Little Mermaid dies. Yes, dies. Worst ending ever. No wonder Hollywood changed it.

"Abby?" Penny asks. "You still there?"

I blink. "Yes! Sorry. Frankie, you read the *Wonderful Wizard of Oz* book, right?"

She nods.

"Does Dotty's house land on the Wicked Witch of the East like it does in the movie?"

"It does," Frankie says. "That part is exactly the same."

Crumbs.

"One difference from the movie," Frankie adds, "is that Dotty sees the witch's *silver* shoes sticking out from underneath the house. Silver slippers. Not ruby ones."

Penny makes a sour face. "Silver shoes? Why'd they change them to ruby?"

"I guess they wanted to make the movie more colorful," Frankie explains. "It was one of the earlier movies filmed in color."

I glance back at Dorothy's house again. "I don't want to worry you all, but I don't see any silver shoes. Or ruby shoes. Could they be under the tree house? We REALLY need those shoes to get home."

"I want to find the shoes!" Penny says. "I'm just gonna circle the house and look for them. I bet they're ruby, though. Silver is just not as cool."

"*I'll* do the circling," I say.

"I got it, Abby," Penny says, hurrying ahead of me.

I chase after her. The last thing I need is Penny finding the shoes before I do and putting them on. What kind of Penny-magic would she try to do? Make sure everyone on the planet wore stain-free T-shirts?

I catch up to her as she turns the corner of the house.

"You better wait for me," I say.

"You're not in charge," Penny says as she hurries by one of the windows.

"Um, yes, I am," I say. "I am absolutely in charge. We're here because of me!"

"Look! Silver shoes!" she cries.

I glance to where Penny is pointing, directly on the grass in front of us, and I gasp. She's right! Sparkly silver shoes!

And there are legs in the shoes. Legs in striped green-and-black tights.

And above the striped tights is a woman in a gray cloak. She has long, knotty silver hair that cascades to her waist and . . . OMG. Just one gray eye in the center of her gray fore-head. So creepy.

She's also holding a broom in one hand and pointing at us with a long, gnarled gray finger.

And she's standing.

And totally alive.

"Um, Abby?" Penny whispers at me. "That's the Wicked Witch of the East, isn't it?"

"I think so," I whisper back, trembling.

"Um, Abby?" Penny says again. "Why isn't the witch under the house?"

"Excellent question," I say.

The wicked witch puts her gnarled hands on her bony hips. "I knew it," she snarls at us. "When I saw that first tiny house falling from the sky, I assumed it was trying to squash me! And I was right. That's what you wanted, wasn't it? And then when your plan failed, you sent another, bigger house down from the sky to get the job done! But see, when that first tiny house fell, I figured out your plan. And I hid! So your second house didn't get me! It landed on the tiny house! You wanted to crush me like a bug. Or a pancake. But your plan failed!"

Crumbs, crumbs, triple crumbs.

"OMW," Penny says under her breath.

"OMW?" I say.

"Oh my witch," Penny exclaims.

OMW is right.

I step forward, trying to keep calm. "We didn't *want* to kill you, Ms. Witch of the East," I say. "We just thought that maybe we *had*. See the difference?"

The witch scowls at us. "Liars!" she snaps.

I want to defend myself, but then I sneeze.

"Curse you!" the witch says. "That's what my sister and I say instead of 'bless you,'" she explains.

"Gee, thanks," I reply, sniffling.

Just then, Robin, Frankie, Prince, and Dorothy run over to us. Dorothy is still clutching Toto. When they see me and Penny facing off with the witch, everyone gasps, and Prince barks worriedly.

"Is that the Wicked Witch of the East?" Frankie asks me. "She's not dead?"

"I thought Dotty killed her," Dorothy says.

"Who's Dotty again?" Robin asks.

"Dotty is Dorothy," Frankie snaps. "C'mon, keep up, Robin."

Gee. What is Frankie's problem today?

"We messed up the story," I rush to tell my friends. "Robin's tree house wasn't supposed to land in Oz. But when it did, the witch saw it fall, and she moved out of the way before Dorothy's house could land on her. And now she's alive. Instead of dead."

Not that we're to blame for landing here. Gluck for sure sent the tornado. He's the one who wants us trapped here. He's the one who messed up the story.

Toto leans his furry head forward and growls at the witch, snapping at her with his little white teeth.

"How dare you, you insolent beast!" the witch yells at him.

"He didn't mean to!" Dorothy says nervously. "He's sorry! He's usually a very good boy!"

Gr-rowl! Prince barks, narrowing his brown eyes at the witch.

"Ugh, your animals are repulsive!" the witch says with a wave of her hand. "I bet they smell, too."

"Hey!" I say defensively. "Prince is NOT smelly. I just gave him a bath!" I look over at Penny to make sure she heard that.

The witch ignores me and claps her hands.

"Munchkins!" she calls.

Suddenly, all the Munchkins who were pretending not to see us earlier appear and start running toward us. How did I not notice before that they were holding spears?

"Yes, Witch?" the Munchkins ask in unison.

"Take these five girls to my castle dungeon," the witch orders, waving her broom. "And their little dogs, too."

Wait, what?

I scoop up Prince and hug him close. The Munchkins surround all of us, looking menacing and pointing their sharp spears in our direction.

"Don't listen to the witch!" I cry out to the Munchkins. "She's evil! Help us instead."

"Take them away immediately," the witch insists.

"Yes, Witch," the Munchkins say in unison.

"Why are they talking to her and not to us?" Penny asks. "Shouldn't they be singing that song? Ding-dong something something?"

"The witch has the Munchkins enslaved," Frankie explains. "They have to do whatever she says. See, in the book, when Dorothy kills the witch with her house, she frees the Munchkins. But now that the witch is alive, they're not free. They still have to do what she says. So they're not singing 'ding-dong, the witch is dead' because —"

"She's not dead," I finish.

"Definitely not dead!" the wicked witch cries out triumphantly. Then she hops on her broom and it shoots straight up into the sky. Whoa. "I'll see you all at my castle!" she shouts down to the Munchkins before flying off into the distance.

"Move it!" one of the Munchkins yells, poking me in the back with a spear.

Ouch.

The other Munchkins poke and prod us until we have no choice but to start marching down the yellow brick road.

"I want to go home," Dorothy announces.

Don't we all.

chapter four

The Dungeon

his way," the Munchkin in front says, twirling the ends of his dark blue mustache.

The Munchkins lead us off the yellow brick road and onto a gray brick road. As we walk, I notice that the bright colors of the grass and flowers and bridges gradually fade away until there's nothing but gray. It's like a rainbow freezie that's had all its juice sucked out, leaving just gray ice. Even the sky has turned gray, but that might be because the sun is setting.

Up ahead, I see a castle come into view. Like everything

else, it's charcoal gray. That must be the witch's castle. Which means we're almost to the dungeon.

Oh, no.

When we reach the gray stone door of the castle, the blue-mustached Munchkin opens the door and orders us all to step inside.

"Can't you just let us go?" I ask the Munchkin. "You can tell the witch we ran away!"

"Are you kidding me?" the Munchkin says. "She's watching us from her window! And besides, we have no choice but to carry out her wishes. As long as she's alive, anyway."

"If only your tree house had landed *on* her," another Munchkin says. "That would have helped a lot."

No kidding.

We follow the blue-mustached Munchkin down a long flight of curving stone steps. Once we're at the bottom, the Munchkin closes the door behind us. We hear it lock.

Crumbs.

Frankie, Penny, Robin, Dorothy, and I all look at one

another in silence. We're in a room with a cement floor and two benches.

But there's another door in the wall! Yay! A way out?

I open it.

No. A small toilet.

Oh, well. At least there's that.

"I wish we could text or call someone for help," Robin says, patting her hoodie pockets. "I left my phone back in my bedroom."

"I have my phone!" Penny says, taking her cell phone out of her back pocket. Then she frowns. "But no service."

I check the time on Penny's phone. Seven P.M. It makes sense that it's seven P.M. here in Oz. But when we were back in Robin's tree house, it was only about two P.M. Penny's phone must have adjusted for the time in Oz.

Time always passes differently in books and stories than it does back home. I have a watch that tracks the correct time back in Smithville, but I forgot to wear it today.

It feels like we've been here in Oz for about an hour, but an hour here could be three hours at home. You never know. Robin's parents could be totally freaking out right now. They could be calling my parents and Frankie's parents and Penny's parents. Or they might not even realize we're gone. Hopefully not that much time has passed back home yet.

I set Prince down and he sniffs at the floor. But Dorothy keeps Toto tight in her arms.

"My aunt and uncle are going to be really worried," she says. "I want to go home!"

"I want to explore Oz," Penny says. "Which I definitely can't do from a dungeon."

And *I* want to get everyone safely out of here before Gluck finds us. And before our parents notice we're missing (along with an entire tree house).

"Frankie?" I say, turning to my friend. She's leaning against the wall and scowling. "We need to know what happens next in the book."

"Who cares what happens?" Penny says, throwing up her hands. "We messed it up. It's not happening anymore!"

"It's still helpful to know," I say. "Trust me. I am the expert in this situation."

"I've been into just as many books as you have," Penny tells me.

"That's ridiculous," I reply. "You have only been in one. I've gone into a dozen fairy tales without you!"

"Fairy *tales*," she says. "Not books. We've both only been inside *one* book. Right?"

My shoulders stiffen. Sure, maybe she's right, technically. But still.

"Guys?" Robin says. "Can you stop fighting?"

I sigh. "Sorry," I say. I turn back to Frankie. "Can you please fill us in on what happens next? We left off when Dorothy —?"

"Dorothy?" Dorothy asks.

"Dotty," I say quickly, "saw the witch and her shoes under the house."

"And then everyone sings!" Penny says.

"In the movie everyone sings," Frankie says. "There's no

45

singing in the book. But that's when the Good Witch of the South, Glinda, shows up. She's nice. She thanks Dotty for killing the evil witch."

"Oh, right," I say. "Glinda! We didn't meet her! I wonder why she didn't come."

Frankie's eyebrows scrunch together. "In the book, the Munchkins send for her after Dotty kills the witch. So since the witch never died, they never sent for her."

"Aha." Foiled again.

"Anyway," Frankie continues, "Glinda is the one who gives Dotty the witch's silver slippers. She tells Dotty to follow the yellow brick road to the Emerald City to ask the Wizard of Oz to send Dotty home. And along the way Dotty meets a scarecrow who wants a brain, a tin man who wants a heart, and a lion who wants courage. Hoping to get these things from the Wizard, they all head to the Emerald City together."

"Do they actually get there?" Robin asks.

Frankie nods. "It takes a while, but yes. When they arrive

in the Emerald City, they ask to see the Wizard. He finally agrees to meet with them one by one. He changes shape for each of them. For Dotty, the Wizard is a big head. For the Lion, he's a terrifying beast. For the Tin Man, he's a beautiful fairy. And for the Scarecrow, he's a big ball of fire. The Wizard tells each of them that to get what he or she wants, they must kill the Wicked Witch of the West."

Dorothy flinches. "This story sounds scary," she says.

"It's a little scary," I admit.

"Wait," Robin says. "I thought you said Dotty's house landed on the witch and killed her?"

"It did," I answer. "But that was the Wicked Witch of the EAST. Now they have to kill her sister — the Wicked Witch of the WEST."

"So violent," Robin says, shivering.

Dorothy crosses her arms. "This story is starting to freak me out."

"Nobody WANTS to kill the witches," I explain. "It's an

accident both times. Dotty kills the second witch when she throws a bucket of water on her and melts her. She had no idea that water killed witches."

"True," Frankie says. "So then the whole group goes back to the Emerald City to tell the Wizard they killed the witch," she continues. "But the Wizard pretty much ignores them. And then Dotty realizes that he's just a fake! He's not really a wizard! He's just a regular person from the Midwest like she is. He's been pretending to have magical powers all that time because he arrived in Oz in a hot-air balloon that crashed and everyone thought he came from the sky. He's just a ventriloquist with really good disguises."

"What's a ventriloquist?" Robin asks.

"Someone who can make their voice sound like it's coming from somewhere else," Frankie explains.

"So there's nothing magical about the Wizard at all," I add. "It's the same in the movie."

Frankie nods. "The Wizard feels bad for pretending. Since the Scarecrow, Tin Man, and Lion still want their

48

wishes granted, he pretends to give the Scarecrow a brain, the Tin Man a heart, and the Lion courage. He tells them he'll make them a hot air balloon to take Dotty home, but the balloon flies off with the Wizard in it. So Dotty visits Glinda the good witch, and Glinda tells Dotty that the silver shoes she was wearing the whole time are magical — all she has to do is tap them together three times and then they'll take her anywhere she wants to go in three steps. And so that's what she does. Dotty says a teary good-bye to her new friends and then takes her steps and suddenly she's back in Kansas with her aunt and uncle, who are excited to see her."

"There's no place like home," I say, remembering the movie with a smile.

Dorothy blinks a bunch of times. "I agree. But . . . Dotty lives with her aunt and uncle in Kansas? *I* live with my aunt and uncle in Kansas!"

"Wow, what a coincidence," I say quickly.

We have to get Dotty — I mean Dorothy — home. We have to get *us* home. But HOW are we going to get out of here?

I crane my neck. I can see windows letting in a little light, but they're very high up, probably at ground level.

I hate dungeons. I really do.

Grr-ruff! Toto growls at Prince.

Grr-ruff! Prince barks back.

"Your dog isn't very nice," Dorothy says, patting Toto.

"Um, your dog growled first," I say.

I wonder if Robin will still want a dog of her own after being locked in a dungeon with two cranky ones.

Dorothy sighs. "Poor Toto just wants to go home. Like I do."

"We know," Frankie snaps. "We want to go home, too, Dorothy. You're not the only one trapped in here."

Robin and I give each other a look. Frankie has been cranky today too. What is up with her?

Dorothy's eyes fill with tears. "There has to be a way out," she says. "We can't be stuck here forever!"

"Do you know what the worst part is?" Penny asks, crossing her arms. "I only have one more piece of gum in my pocket. Since we don't know how long we're going to be here, I don't know if I should chew it now or save it."

"Yeah, that's a real dilemma," Frankie says, rolling her eyes.

A cold blast of air suddenly fills the dungeon. What is that? The windows aren't open. If they were, we could sneak out.

"Is there a ghost in the story?" Robin asks, wrapping her arms around herself.

"No," Frankie says, her teeth chattering.

My teeth chatter, too, and I sneeze again. Ugh. This freezing temperature can't be good for me if I'm getting sick.

Then the cold air is gone as quickly as it came. That was weird. Broken air vent?

"Okay," I say. "Let's brainstorm. Clearly we need to get the witch's silver shoes. Once we have them, we can use them to go home. Right?" I look at Frankie.

She nods. "That makes sense to me."

"But how do we get the shoes?" Penny asks. "Since they're otherwise occupied."

"Do you mean they're on the witch's feet?" Robin asks.

Frankie rolls her eyes again. "Of course that's what she meant."

Robin blushes.

I give Frankie a what-is-going-on-with-you? look, but she ignores me and says, "Anyway, the answer is clear."

It is?

"It is?" Penny asks.

"Yes," Frankie says. "Remember how Dorothy accidentally threw water on the witch and killed her?"

"I did?" Dorothy asks. "No, I didn't! I thought Dotty threw water on the mean witch?"

"OMG, Dorothy, there is no Dotty!" Frankie yells. "There is a book — no, a whole series written about you and what happens to you in Oz, and that's what we're talking about, okay?"

"Frankie!" I cry. "We can't say stuff like that! It messes up the stories!"

"The story is already pretty messed up," she points out.

True.

Dorothy's lower lip quivers. "But . . . but . . . what does that mean? I'm just a character in a book?"

Crumbs.

"Does that mean I'm not even real?" She looks down at her little black dog. "That Toto isn't even real?"

"Exactly," Frankie says, just as I say, "It's complicated."

Robin puts her arm around Dorothy. "She feels real," she says. She tickles Dorothy's waist. Dorothy laughs.

"See? She even laughed," Robin says.

"She's real enough," I say, and turn back to Frankie. "Can you stop freaking out the characters and just tell us your plan to get us the silver shoes?"

Frankie shrugs. "It's so obvious. We dump a glass of water on the witch's head. Then we take the shoes off her feet."

We all gasp.

"You want us to kill someone?" Robin exclaims.

It does seem a little extreme.

"Abby, you said you wanted to keep the story intact,"

Frankie says. "And that's what Dorothy did in the story. She killed both witches! So why shouldn't she do it now?"

Frankie has a point, but it still feels wrong. "The house landing on the witch was an accident," I say. "So was throwing water on the witch. Well, Dorothy threw the water at the witch on purpose, but she had no idea it would make her melt."

"I guess," Frankie says.

"Let's just focus on getting the magic shoes," Penny says.

"Don't even bother," a voice says. And we all freeze.

chapter five

Outsmarting the Witch

I look at Frankie, Robin, Penny, and Dorothy. That wasn't any of their voices.

It didn't sound like the witch's voice, either. But it *did* come from the other side of the dungeon door.

There's a small window in the door, and when I look through, I see a skinny Munchkin girl in a blue dress and pointy purple shoes. She has long curly blue hair and blue lip gloss. At least she's not carrying a spear.

"Oh, hi," I say. "We didn't know you were there!"

"Sorry," the Munchkin says, waving. "I didn't mean to surprise you. Or be all negative. But it's hard to be positive when you constantly have to do things against your better judgment."

"What do you mean?" Robin asks, coming to stand beside me.

"All us Munchkins are magically enslaved by the wicked witch," she explains. "We hate her. But we have to do what she says even though we don't want to."

Right.

"That must be hard," I say.

"It is!" she says with a nod, her curly hair bouncing on her shoulders. "I'm Orly. The dungeon guard. And I really feel bad about you girls — and dogs — being locked down here."

"I'm Abby," I say. "And this is Robin, Frankie, and Penny. And that's Dorothy in the blue-and-white dress. Oh, and this is Prince," I say, giving Prince's paw a little wave. "And that dog in Dorothy's arms is Toto."

Toto barks.

"Orly?" Robin asks through the door. "Since the witch isn't here, maybe you can just open the door with your key and let us out? Dorothy really wants to go home. We all do."

Orly shakes her head. "Wish I could," she says. "But you'll have to come up with a plan that doesn't include me."

"I have an idea," Penny says, coming over to the door, too. "We wait until the witch falls asleep and then swipe her magic silver shoes."

"Impossible," Orly says. "The witch sleeps in them!"

Oh. Of course she does.

"How about when she's taking a shower?" Robin asks.

"Water makes her melt," I say. "She probably doesn't shower."

"She definitely doesn't shower," Orly says. "She is super stinky."

"Ew!" Penny exclaims, holding her nose. "That sounds even worse than a smelly dog."

"Dogs are not smelly," I protest.

Ruff! Prince barks, as if in agreement. *Ruff, ruff!*

Penny sighs. She kicks off one of her sneakers and wiggles her big toe. "I think I'm getting a blister."

Toto whimpers.

"Aww, Toto, it's okay," Dorothy coos to him. "We'll be home soon. And we'll run around the prairie and have all sorts of fun and play fetch!"

As soon as Dorothy says "fetch," Toto springs out of her arms. He and Prince both make a run for Penny's loose shoe. Prince grabs it in his mouth and charges back across the room.

"Hey! Stop that, mutt!" Penny cries to Prince.

"Sorry," I say. "Dorothy said 'fetch.'"

"He better give me back my shoe," Penny says. She hops over to Prince, holding her bare foot off the ground. "Bad dog! Bad dog!"

"He didn't know," I say. "Prince, drop the shoe."

Prince drops it and Penny picks it up. "Ew. It's wet. My fancy new sneaker!"

It's just a shoe. It's not like it has magic powers or anything. Unless . . .

"Penny!" I exclaim. "You have fancy new sneakers!"

"Yes," she says. "I do. Correction, I have fancy new sneakers that are now covered in dog slobber."

I ignore the comment. "What if we convinced the witch that your sneakers are magical? That they are even *more* magical than her silver slippers? And then somehow get her to trade her shoes with yours?"

"I don't want to give up my new shoes!" Penny protests, putting the slobbery shoe back on.

"It's a good plan," Frankie says.

Penny sticks out her feet, showing her shoes off to everyone. "I guess they'd be worth trading for ruby slippers . . . and I can always get another pair of these. Ruby slippers are one in a million."

"Silver slippers," I correct.

"Why do they call them slippers?" Robin asks. "They're not bunny slippers."

"I think it's just another word for *shoes*," I explain hastily. "And we need them to get us out of here."

"Yay, I'm getting the magic slippers!" Penny exclaims.

"Dorothy is," I say.

"It doesn't have to be Dorothy," Penny says. "Any of us could wear the slippers."

I roll my eyes. "But Dorothy is the one who ends up with the shoes in the story."

"But I'll be the one giving up *my* shoes," Penny says.

We can argue technicalities later.

I look out the door window again. "Orly, could you summon the witch for us?"

Orly shakes her head. "She always ignores us Munchkins when we ask to see her." Her eyes light up. "But I know how you can do it."

"How?" I ask.

"Remember how cold it got in here before?" Orly says.

"Yeah," I say.

"Well, every so often, the witch will spy on you down here in the dungeon using her magic ball. If it gets really cold in here, that's how you know she's watching!"

"So how does that help us?" Robin asks.

"When you know the witch is watching," Orly says, "start talking about how magical and special Penny's shoes are. She'll want them. Trust me, she'll want them."

"Perfect," I say.

"Not really," Frankie says. "Wouldn't she realize that if Penny's shoes were really magical, we'd be out of here by now?"

I instantly deflate. Frankie's right.

"Although maybe the witch isn't that smart," Robin says. "And what other options do we have?"

A cold blast of air suddenly fills the dungeon. The witch is listening! It's now or never! I glance around the room. Everyone nods.

Here goes nothing.

"Penny," I say — loudly. "Your checkered sneakers are so cool!" My voice sounds super fake.

"I was with Penny when she bought them in the magic shop," Frankie shouts. "The salesclerk said whoever wears them will have the power to read minds!"

"Yup," Penny adds, cupping her hands around her mouth as if speaking through a megaphone. "And they can turn you invisible if you give your feet a little stomp."

"They were, um, really expensive," Robin adds. "But so worth it for all their amazing powers!"

"Too bad the magic powers don't kick in until whoever has them on has worn them for six hours," Frankie adds.

Smart! "That's right," I say. "Penny's only had them on for three hours."

"Because I bought them . . . this morning," Penny says.

"So the magic won't work for a little while," I add.

Is this starting to sound ridiculous? I think it is.

"I wish I had a pair of magic black-and-white-checkered sneakers," Dorothy yells with a grin, catching on. Go, Dorothy!

"Do you know that once you've been wearing the shoes for six hours, you can turn vegetables into candy?" Robin asks.

"And tissues into dollar bills!" Penny adds.

Now we're definitely pushing it.

"These are one-of-a-kind shoes," I say, wanting to wrap it up before my friends go too far. "And the only pair in existence are on Penny's feet!"

The cold air goes away as suddenly as it came.

Ah.

Which means the witch has stopped listening. Did we do a convincing enough job?

We all wait.

"Out of the way, Munchkin!" shouts a distant voice.

YES! It's the witch! Her voice is coming from up the stairs.

The door creaks open and we all turn as the witch stomps into the dungeon.

The witch focuses her one eye on Penny. "You. Give me your shoes. Now."

Penny smiles triumphantly. "Sure. I'll switch with you."

Hurrah! My plan worked! I was truly worried the witch wouldn't be dumb enough to fall for it!

The witch points her gnarled finger in Penny's face. "Who said anything about switching?" the witch snaps.

Penny puts her hands on her hips. "Well, I can't go around shoeless! Especially in this dungeon. The floor is concrete."

"You give me the shoes," the witch snarls, "or I will zap you into oblivion and take them."

Yikes.

Penny slips off her shoes.

"Wise," the witch says, her voice dripping with menace. She snatches up the sneakers and slams the door behind her.

Crumbs.

"I hope they're too small on her and give her blisters," Penny mutters, glaring at me. "Great idea, *Abby*!"

My cheeks heat up. "It almost worked," I say.

But *almost* isn't getting us out of this dungeon.

Now what?

"Okay, I have another idea," Penny says.

"What?" I ask.

"Let's ask Orly to steal the witch's magic shoes for us!" Penny says.

I see Orly's face pop up into the window.

"Sorry, but I can't," Orly says. "The magic spell that enslaves the Munchkins would not allow it."

"Oh, yeah," Penny says, her shoulders slumping.

"I'm about to go on my evening snack break," Orly says. "I'm sorry I can't help you. I wish I could. All I can say is that it's a good thing the witch didn't ask me to lock the door when she left. Because then I would have had to lock the door."

"Wait. Are you saying what I think you're saying?" I ask.

"I don't know what you're talking about," Orly calls out.

I turn to my friends. "The door is unlocked!"

"Let's go!" Dorothy cries.

"You should know the witch will go to sleep at nine P.M. exactly," Orly adds. "She'll be sleeping in the new sneakers, I suppose. And the magic slippers will be right by her bed. I'm just mentioning these details in case you're curious."

I give Orly a thumbs-up through the glass. "Thank you for letting us know. But you won't get in trouble?"

"I follow orders. She didn't tell me to lock the door. I did nothing wrong."

"Thank you, Orly!" I say.

She winks.

chapter six

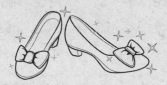

These Shoes Are Made
for Walking

We wait in the dungeon. As soon as the time on Penny's phone switches to nine P.M., we jump up, ready to go.

"What's our plan here, exactly?" Frankie asks.

Oh. Good point. We don't really have a fully formed plan yet.

"Well, we all leave the dungeon," I say. "You guys hide somewhere safe. Meanwhile, I go into the witch's room and get the shoes."

"You?" Penny cries. "*I'll* get the shoes."

"No, I'll get them," I say. "I'm the expert."

"You are not," she says. "We've both been in the same number of books! C'mon! And anyway, she stole *my* shoes! I'm going."

"Why do you want to go so badly?" I ask her. "You understand it's dangerous, right?"

"It's not that dangerous. It's exciting!"

"Two people *should* go," Frankie says. "One to be the lookout, one to grab the shoes."

Crumbs. She's right.

"Fine," I say. "Penny and I can go. The rest of you go hide somewhere safe. In case we get caught, you'll have to save us."

"Can't I just go straight home?" Dorothy asks.

"You will when we get those silver shoes," I promise her.

"We need a meeting spot," Frankie says. "So Abby and Penny can find us after they're done getting the shoes."

"How about back where we first landed?" I suggest.

Frankie nods. "Okay. We'll start walking toward there — maybe you'll catch up with us along the way."

"You'll take Prince?" I ask Robin.

"Of course," she says, scooping him up and nuzzling his fur.

I give Prince a fast scratch under the chin. "You be a good boy for Robin."

He licks my hand.

"Ew," Penny whispers. "Dog slobber."

I roll my eyes. "Let's go."

I carefully open the door, and we all go racing out and up the stairs. Dorothy, Frankie, and Robin wave to me and Penny, and then they slip out the main castle door into the night. I feel a tiny lump in my throat. I hope Prince will be okay! I trust Robin, but still.

Everything is quiet and dark. There's no one around in the castle. Not a Munchkin in sight. Or the witch.

"We have to find the witch's bedroom," I whisper to Penny. I wish we'd asked Orly where it is. Too late.

Penny and I tiptoe around the corner and down the first hall. I see two doors. One says WITCH'S PRIVATE QUARTERS. Um, guessing it's that one.

Penny and I tiptoe to the door and I open it very, very carefully.

The door opens without a creak.

Whew.

I peer into the witch's bedroom. There's a big four-poster gray stone bed in the center of the room. The witch's head is at the far end, atop three lumpy-looking gray pillows. The rest of her is covered by a scratchy gray blanket.

And her feet are sticking right out of the blanket! And she's wearing Penny's sneakers! Just like Orly said she would be.

Penny creeps right over to the witch and reaches out to snatch the shoes off her feet.

You'll wake her up! I mouth.

But I want my shoes! she mouths back.

I shake my head no.

She hesitates. "So then I get to wear the ruby slippers?" she whispers.

So annoying. "Silver slippers. But fine. If we find them," I whisper back. I glance around the room. There's not much in here. Just a bedside table with a lamp.

But underneath the table? I squint. Could it be? The silver slippers!

Yes!

I tiptoe toward them.

I reach out. I grab. I have them! "Got 'em!" I whisper-shout.

Penny smiles. And then grabs them right out of my hands!

She goes running out of the room, her feet still bare. I follow, taking a peek back at the witch. She hasn't woken up. Thank goodness.

I gently close the door behind us. Penny puts on the shoes.

"OMG, how cute and sparkly are these?" she asks.

They *are* cute and sparkly. They have a small heel and glitter like they're made of diamonds. I wish I was wearing them.

"They fit me perfectly," Penny adds. "What are the chances?"

"Well, they *are* magic," I grumble. "Let's get out of here before the witch wakes up."

We retrace our steps and slip out of the stone front door.

Then we race as fast as we can away from the witch's castle, down the gray brick road back toward the yellow brick road.

I see a light on the ground. I glance at it — it's Penny's phone. She's put the flashlight app on. Good thinking.

"Let's see where we are," Penny says, and shines the light ahead of us.

Dorothy's fallen house is right in front of us. With, I'm guessing, Robin's tree house crunched under it.

"Guys!" I whisper-yell, looking for our friends. "Are you here?"

No answer.

"Guys?" I say again.

I hope nothing happened to them. Where are they?

Suddenly, I feel a lick on my leg. I jump. It's Prince!

"Hi!" I say, bending down and scratching behind his ears. "You're okay! Yay! Where's everyone else?"

"We're here," Robin says, stepping forward out of the darkness with Frankie and Dorothy.

"Did you get the shoes?" Frankie asks me and Penny.

"Yes!" Penny says. "And they're amazing!"

She preens in her fancy footwear so everyone can see. The moonlight over this part of Oz is bright.

"Can we go home now?" Dorothy asks, hugging Toto.

"Yes!" I say. Dorothy and I are one hundred percent on the same page. We're just two girls with dogs who want to go home! "I think we should leave here as soon as possible. So nobody gets hurt."

"How are we getting home exactly?" Frankie asks. "We only have one pair of slippers."

"Maybe if we all hold hands it will work?" I say.

"But what if we get stuck in Kansas?" Penny says. "Or Dorothy gets stuck in Smithville?"

"That would not be ideal," Frankie says.

"But as long as we have the shoes, we can get anywhere," I say. "So maybe Dorothy puts them on, like she's supposed to, and we all hold hands and we fly over to Kansas and drop off Dorothy. And then I put the shoes on and we do the same to get back to Smithville."

"Or, you know, I could put them back on," Penny says casually.

"We'll see," I say. We will not see.

"But what about the rest of the story?" Penny adds. "What about the Scarecrow, the Tin Man, and the Lion? If we leave now, Dorothy will never meet them and they'll never get a brain, a heart, or courage!"

"But they don't really get them anyway," Frankie explains. "The Wizard of Oz is a fake. He just pretends to give them a brain, a heart, and courage. Remember? Didn't you listen when I explained before?"

Penny frowns. "Yeah, but I don't agree. Anyway, doesn't Dorothy still set the Scarecrow free? And oil the Tin Man? If she doesn't help them, they'll be stuck forever!" She glances at me. "Plus, wouldn't it be cool to meet them all?"

"Penny, you don't realize how much danger we're in," I say. "In the book, Dorothy had only one witch after her. We have two! Plus Gluck!"

"Who's Gluck again?" Robin asks, scrunching her face. "I can't keep this story straight."

"Gluck isn't in the real story, he's in *my* story," I say.

"Now I'm even more confused," Robin says.

"Me too," says Dorothy.

"Gluck is after me," I say. "He is trying to trap me here so I don't help the fairy in my basement. And he's dangerous."

Toto starts to whimper again. Prince barks at him.

"I'm in charge," I say loudly. "And it's my decision. We're going home. We can't risk it. Penny, give Dorothy the shoes."

"But they fit me perfectly! And I'm already wearing them."

"Can you just listen to me for once?" I sigh.

"Fine," Penny grumbles. "You're so bossy, Abby."

Dorothy undoes the buckle on her clunky white shoes and passes them to Penny.

"These are pretty ugly," Penny says, handing over the silver slippers.

"Hey! That's not very nice," says Dorothy.

"Well, it's true. It's my job to point out fashion mistakes," Penny says. "And these are two of them."

Seriously, Penny? I shake my head.

Dorothy puts on the silver slippers. "How do they look?" she asks.

"They look great," Penny mutters. "Obviously, they look great. Although the color really *is* boring."

"So what do I have to do with the shoes again?" Dorothy asks.

"Okay," I say. "What you have to do is —"

The strangest sound fills the night sky.

WAA-WEE! WAA-WEE!

What. Is. That?

We look all around. I don't see anything.

WAA-WEE!

Prince's ears flatten. So do Toto's. They're both staring up at the sky.

We all look up.

In the moonlight we see . . . monkeys?

With wings?

Flying monkeys!

Furry brown monkeys with wings are flying through the sky. There are at least ten of them.

"AHHHHHHH!" Penny cries. "AHHHHHH! The flying monkeys! I forgot about the flying monkeys! Don't let them get me, don't let them get me!"

"Run!" I shout. "Hide!"

But before any of us can move, two monkeys swoop down. One grabs Dorothy by the collar of her dress. Toto falls out of her arms and barks up at Dorothy from the ground.

"Totooooooo!" Dorothy cries as the monkey carries her up, up, and away.

They have Dorothy! And the magic shoes!

The other flying monkey lunges for me, but I duck, and the monkey heads straight for Robin.

"What is *that*?" Robin screams. "None of you mentioned flying monkeys!"

The monkey grabs her by her hoodie and swoops her up and away.

Oh, noooooo.

The monkeys have Dorothy *and* Robin!

The monkeys are carrying them higher and higher and farther and farther away!

Prince and Toto are barking loudly and spinning in circles.

"HAHAHAHAHA!" a male voice calls down.

What? The monkeys can talk?

I stare up at the flying monkey who's carrying Robin. Its face suddenly changes before my eyes. It's becoming . . . human. Ice-blue eyes. A turned-up nose. Thin lips. And white-blond hair.

I know that face!

It's Gluck! The evil fairy! I *knew* he was behind this. And now he stole Robin!

We all stare up at the dark sky. The monkeys are gone. The magic shoes are gone.

And so are our friends.

chapter seven

Brainless

We have to save Robin and Dorothy!" I cry. They must be terrified. Robin is one of my best friends — the thought of anything bad happening to her is beyond awful. And I feel totally responsible for Dorothy. We messed up her story, and now she's been kidnapped. BY FLYING MONKEYS! Oh, and by Gluck, the evil fairy. Not good. Not good at all.

"The monkeys. The monkeys. The monkeys," Penny

keeps repeating. She's hugging herself and rocking back and forth. "I forgot about the monkeys."

Toto is wailing.

Prince is barking.

Frankie is just shaking her head. "Where would the Winged Monkeys take them?" she asks. "That's what they're called in the books. Winged. Not flying."

"Who cares what they're called?" Penny says, still shivering. "They're horrifying."

I think. Hard. "Well, since the monkeys work for the Wicked Witch of the West," I say, "they probably took Robin and Dorothy to the witch's castle. That's what happened in the movie. Is that what happened in the book?"

Frankie nods. "So we'll have to go to the witch's castle."

"*Back* to the castle?" Penny groans. "We just came from there!"

I shake my head. "The castle we just came from belongs to the Wicked Witch of the *East*. The Wicked Witch of the *West* is her sister. She's an entirely different witch."

Penny sighs. "So many witches. So many directions!"

"I know," I say.

"But Dorothy is wearing the shoes," Penny says. "Can't she just click her heels together and take herself back to Kansas?"

"Let's hope she doesn't do that," I say. "If she leaves with the shoes, *we* might be stuck here for good. Plus, Dorothy might leave Robin behind, and we still need to save her." I clap my hands. "Come on. Time to go!"

"Wait. You want to go *chase* the flying monkeys?" Penny asks. "Are you joking? I am not going near those things!"

"We don't have much of a choice," I say.

Penny shudders. "But . . . but . . . I had nightmares about those monkeys when I was a kid, after I saw the movie! I . . . I want to go home!"

"So do I. But first we have to save our friends," I say.

"I wish we'd never come into this story!" she says.

Toto gives another wail.

Prince sidles up beside him and rubs his nose against

Toto's neck. Aw, cute. He's trying to cheer him up. What a good dog. I turn back to Penny.

"I told you the stories aren't all fun and games," I say. "Now, we have to figure out where this castle is, exactly. Frankie, any ideas?"

She shakes her head.

"Where is Glinda when we need her?" Penny huffs. She fiddles with her phone. "Can't we call her?"

"I don't know how to do that," I say.

"Maybe we can ask the Scarecrow or the Tin Man or the Lion," Frankie says. "They might know how to find Glinda. Or, even better, show us the way to the witch's castle."

"You're right!" I say, feeling a flash of hope. "And remember how Dorothy found the Scarecrow, the Tin Man, and the Lion? All we have to do is follow the yellow brick road."

Penny, Frankie, and I start walking down the road, with Toto and Prince on our heels.

"Should we sing that 'follow the yellow brick road' song?" Penny says, perking up.

"I'm not singing," Frankie snaps.

"Okay, Cranky Frankie," Penny mutters. "What's wrong with you today?"

Good question.

"Our friends were just kidnapped by Winged Monkeys," Frankie says, crossing her arms while she walks. "We shouldn't be singing!"

"Well, I want to sing," Penny says, and clears her throat. *"Follow the yellow brick road. Follow the yellow brick road . . ."*

I jump in. *"Follow, follow, follow, follow, follow the yellow brick road!"*

"Are you guys trying to get caught by Winged Monkeys yourselves?" Frankie snaps. "Don't we want to be quiet?"

Fair point.

We walk in silence.

We follow the yellow brick road, and follow, follow, follow, but we do it very quietly.

Luckily the moonlight is bright so we can see where we're going.

"Look," Penny says, pointing. "Cornfields!"

"The Scarecrow should be around here somewhere," I say, stopping in place.

We glance around in every direction.

"Prince, do you see him?" I ask, scratching my dog behind the ears. "Find the Scarecrow!"

"How would he know what a scarecrow is?" Penny asks.

"He's a very smart dog," I say.

Prince darts off. Toto stays with us.

Soon, we hear barking.

"This way!" I say, and we all run to where Prince is barking.

"Penny," I say. "Can you shine your phone's flashlight over there?"

Penny pulls her phone out of her pocket and shines it around where Prince is standing. The light illuminates a pair of blue boots. Penny shines it higher up. Blue pants. Blue shirt. Burlap-sack arms sticking out of the sleeves. And the head is a burlap sack stuffed with something. There's a face painted on — blue eyes and a blue nose and a blue smiling mouth. On top of his head is a pointy blue hat, the kind the Munchkins wear, but this one is old and tattered. Straw pokes out of the burlap arms. And he seems to be stuck on some kind of a pole wedged into the ground.

I gasp.

It's the Scarecrow.

"Hi, Scarecrow!" I say. "Nice to meet you!"

I don't expect him to answer me, but he does. His head turns toward me and his eyes seem to light up a little. It would almost be scary, except I know the Scarecrow is nice.

"Do I know you?" he asks in a scratchy voice.

"No. But we know you," Frankie says.

"You do?" he asks. "How?"

"You're famous," I say.

"You're looking for a brain," Penny adds.

"Hey!" Scarecrow says, pursing his lips. "That's not nice. It's true, but not nice. Can you help me get a brain?"

"Yes!" Penny says, just as I say, "No."

"Why not?" Penny asks me.

"Because we need to rescue Robin and Dorothy and then we need to go home," I say. "We're not going to meet the Wizard."

"Wizard?" Scarecrow asks. "There's a wizard? What wizard? I want to meet a wizard!"

"The Wizard of Oz. He can give you a brain," Penny says.

"There's a wizard who can get me a brain?" Scarecrow cheers. "Hurrah! Best wizard ever!"

"He can't *really* give you a brain," Frankie says. "He's a fraud."

Scarecrow squirms on his pole. "Why don't you get me down, and then we can discuss this properly?"

"Yes!" I say. "Sorry. That we can do."

We help him down. He's pretty light, which makes sense since he's made of straw. The second his feet touch the ground, he takes a step.

"I can walk!" Scarecrow says. He puts one arm around me and one around Frankie to help him balance. His legs are wobbling, though.

"Scarecrow, do you know where the Wicked Witch of the West's castle is?" I ask.

He throws his head back and laughs. "No! Why would I know that? I live in a cornfield!"

Crumbs.

"So what do we do now?" I ask Frankie and Penny.

"We go see this Wizard," Scarecrow says.

"We're not seeing the Wizard," I say. "We have to find our friends. Who are at the witch's castle. Which we don't know the location of. Who else might know?"

"The Tin Man!" Penny says. "I bet he would know."

"She's right," Frankie says. "We keep going down the yellow brick road. And hope we find the Tin Man."

chapter eight

Heartless

d o you see the Tin Man?" I ask.

"No," Frankie says.

"Me neither," Penny says. She is using the flashlight on her phone to light up the yellow brick road.

Scarecrow is on the lookout, too. His legs are still wobbling, but at least he's standing on his own two feet.

We've been walking for at least an hour. I'm getting really worried about Dorothy and Robin.

Please, please, please, let them be okay.

Prince is leading our pack, and Toto is behind him, still whimpering.

"What's wrong, little man?" Scarecrow asks Toto.

"He doesn't talk," I say.

"Oh!" Scarecrow says, looking surprised. "Interesting!"

Another whimper.

"Is he ever going to stop crying?" Penny moans.

"Probably when we find Dorothy," Frankie says. "He did just see his best friend get abducted by Winged Monkeys."

"Oh, I remember," Penny says, angling the flashlight into the forest again. Suddenly, the light bounces back to us.

"What was that?" I ask.

Prince bolts off the yellow brick road and into the forest.

"Prince, wait!" I cry, heading after him.

Ruff! I hear him bark.

Penny and Frankie follow me into the forest.

"Scarecrow, stay there with Toto!" I call out.

It's so dark I can barely see. I try to avoid running head-first into a tree or tripping over one of the roots.

PLUNK!

I run right into something. Something HARD. I stumble backward and land on my butt.

"Oi," a very creaky voice says.

I jump up. That was a man's voice!

I swallow. "Um, who said that?"

"Oi. Yul," the voice croaks out.

Oi. Yul. What is Oi Yul?

Penny shines her phone flashlight ahead.

The light shines on what looks like a foot.

Penny raises the flashlight slowly. The foot leads to a silver leg. A silver body. A silver head, and a frowning face.

"Tin Man?" I ask. "Is that you?"

"AHHHHHHH!" Penny screams. "Ahhhhhhh!"

"What's wrong?" I ask.

"He's holding an ax!" she says.

"He's supposed to be," Frankie says. "He cuts wood! That's his job!"

Penny shines the light over him. He's frozen in place. "Why isn't he moving?"

"Because he's rusty," Frankie explains. "He needs his —"

"Oi . . . yul," he repeats.

"Oil!" Frankie says. "He needs the jug of oil. Everyone look for the jug! Penny, shine your flashlight on the ground!"

"Witch," he says slowly. "Cursed. Tin."

"Where is the can?" I ask. "I'll get it for you!"

"Tree," he barely manages to say.

I run over to a nearby tall, thin tree.

I look behind the tree and find Prince sniffing the oil can. Good dog. The can has a silver spout. I grab it and rush back over to Tin Man.

"I'll do that!" Penny says, grabbing the can out of my hand.

"I got it," I say, trying to grab it back.

"I'll do it," Frankie snaps, grabbing the can from both our hands.

"Whatever, Cranky Frankie," Penny mutters.

Frankie ignores her and pours the oil from the spout into Tin Man's mouth and then into the joints of Tin Man's arms.

"Ahhh," he says with relief, bending his elbows. "Yay! So much better. Thank you!"

Frankie continues oiling his joints until Tin Man can move all his limbs. "Did I get everything?" she asks.

He puts down the ax and stretches his metal arms above his head. "You did! I feel great now. I haven't felt this good in years! Thank you for rescuing me!"

"You're welcome," Frankie says.

"Is there anything I can do to return the favor?" he asks.

"Yes, actually," I say. "Do you happen to know where the Wicked Witch of the West's castle is? We need to find it."

"I do!" he says. "Do you really want to go there, though? She's horrible."

"We know," I say. "She kidnapped our friends."

"She put a curse on me," he says, cringing. "That's why I'm made of tin."

"Why would she do that?" Penny asks.

"I fell in love with a nice young woman and the witch got very jealous," he explains. "She didn't want us to be together. And so she stuck me out here, unable to move."

"But now you can move," Penny says. "Are you going to find the nice young woman?"

He shakes his head sadly. "No point in that," he says. "I'm made out of tin. I don't have a heart. I can't love anyone."

"You poor guy," I say.

"So does that mean you'll come with us?" Penny asks. "To save our friends?"

"He doesn't have to," I say quickly. "We can't offer him a heart in return, like Dorothy did in the movie."

"Of course I'll come," he says, squaring his metal shoulders. "You just saved me from an eternity of rusting in the forest. And it's not like I have any other big plans tonight."

"Great," Penny says. "We could use the backup!"

We lead Tin Man back through the forest and to the yellow brick road, where Scarecrow is waiting patiently with Toto.

"Tin Man, meet Scarecrow and Toto!" I say. "Toto and Scarecrow, meet Tin Man."

Scarecrow extends his hand to Tin Man.

"Nice to meet you!" Scarecrow says.

"The pleasure is all mine!" says Tin Man.

Okay, I have to admit. It's super fun to meet the characters from the story. Maybe Penny was right.

"Are you coming along to the witch's castle?" Tin Man asks Scarecrow.

"Me?" Scarecrow says. "No! Why would I do that?"

"They need to save their friends," Tin Man explains, gesturing to me, Frankie, Penny, and the dogs.

"In that case, of course," Scarecrow says.

These guys are the best.

"Do we just take the yellow brick road all the way there?" Frankie asks Tin Man.

"Oh, no," he says. "The yellow brick road goes to the Emerald City. It doesn't go to the wicked witch's castle. We have to go through the Dark Scary Forest to get to the castle."

"That's not really what it's called, is it?" Penny asks.

"It totally is," Tin Man says. "Although Ozonians call it the DSF for short."

Great.

"Let's go," Frankie commands, lifting her chin and leading the way. "We want to get there while it's still night. Easier to hide in the dark."

"Yeah," Penny snorts. "Let's go walk through the DSF to storm a witch's castle filled with flying monkeys in the middle of the night. What could go wrong?"

"Can you stop whining?" Frankie asks.

"Okay, Cranky Frankie," Penny says.

Frankie turns and narrows her eyes at Penny.

"Maybe we'll find the Lion," I say. "Remember the Lion? He's roaming around the forest somewhere. He can help us take on the witches!"

"You want us to run into a lion in the middle of the night in the forest?" Scarecrow asks. "Are you sure? Lions eat humans, you know."

"This lion won't eat us," I say. "He's kind of a scaredy-cat."

"Then how will he help us against the witches?" Tin Man asks.

"Good point," Penny says.

It's not just the witches, either. It's the witches plus Gluck.

I take a deep breath. This is going to be a long night.

chapter nine

Quick as a Wink

We walk for an hour through the Dark Scary Forest. Unfortunately — or fortunately — we don't meet the Lion.

But then —

"Look!" Frankie exclaims, pointing up ahead. "The witch's castle!"

Beyond a cluster of trees, I can make out a looming gray castle. It looks even scarier than the other witch's castle.

Our whole crew makes our way toward it. The scenery

around us gets grayer as we get closer. The leaves are gray. The grass is gray. Even the flowers are gray. Who even knew gray flowers existed?

Tin Man creaks as he walks, and Scarecrow's legs are still a bit jellyish, but we all make it. We stop in front of the stone wall that surrounds the castle.

"Should we storm it?" Tin Man asks.

"No," I say. "We should figure out where everyone is."

"Like the flying monkeys. I do not need to see them ever again," Penny says.

She glances up at the sky, swallows, and moves behind Tin Man.

"I've been turned into tin by this witch," Tin Man says. "But I'm not afraid of her or her minions!"

"That makes one of us," Penny says. Then she yelps. "Did anyone else see that?"

We look to where she's pointing. On the other side of the wall, something yellow just ran by in a blur.

"That was a Winkie," Frankie says. "And look, there are more."

About twenty little people in yellow clothcs march by.

"*Who* are they?" Scarecrow asks.

"Winkies," Frankie repeats. "They had their own area of Oz, but then the Wicked Witch of the West enslaved them like the Wicked Witch of the East enslaved the Munchkins."

Tin Man nods. "It's so sad. The Winkies were nice till the witch got ahold of them. Now they're guards."

"So how are we getting past them?" Penny asks.

I think about that. "I can try to slip past them on my own," I say. "I'm used to this kind of stuff."

"Scarecrow and I will come along to help save your friends," Tin Man says, standing up tall.

That sure is nice of him, for someone who doesn't have a heart. But Tin Man is still too creaky and Scarecrow still isn't walking perfectly.

"You guys are kind of hard to miss," I point out. "I think I should go on my own. Or with one other person. Maybe since Frankie knows the story, she stays here with you guys and the dogs, and Penny comes with me? That might be useful if Penny and I get caught."

Penny's eyes widen. "You want me to go with you?"

"Yeah?" I say.

"To where the flying monkeys are?"

"Yes?"

"Um, hard pass," she says. "Sorry. I can't. I just can't."

"Penny!" I cry. "We have to save Robin and Dorothy!"

"I get it but . . . no. Let Frankie do it!" She shudders.

"I'll go with you," Frankie says. "That's fine with me. Penny can babysit the dogs and characters."

"We're not just *characters*," Tin Man says. "We're people, too."

"I'm not really a person," Scarecrow says. "I'm made of straw. But I appreciate the support."

I turn to Frankie. "Do you think we should go around the side to avoid the Winkies? Maybe there's a door or a window we can sneak into?"

Toto cries again. Prince barks at him.

"Shush!" Penny says. "You're going to get them caught!"

Toto starts crying even louder.

"Maybe pick him up?" I suggest.

"Gross," she says, making a face. But she picks him up. "Stop crying! They're going to get Dorothy back for you."

Toto seems to understand that, and quiets.

"You guys stay hidden behind this wall," I say. The wall is about a hundred feet from the castle.

They nod. I kiss Prince good-bye-for-now, then grab Frankie's hand, and we go darting behind the trees to the edge of the castle. I peer around a tall gray tree. There's a small oval door and it's not guarded. Two Winkies with pointy yellow shoes and yellow hats are sitting on a nearby bench. They're chatting while they share a small pepperoni pizza.

Mmm. I'm hungry.

If we can just slip behind them, we can try the door to see if it's unlocked.

"On my count of three, let's tiptoe over to the door," I say.

Frankie nods. "We got this. Penny may be a coward, but I'm not!"

Kind of mean, but I do need her to be brave.

"One, two, threeeeee!" I whisper-yell, then grab her hand and go running for the entrance to the castle.

We made it! We're at the door. Now we just have to very quietly turn the handle. I put my hand on it. I turn it . . .

My nose is starting to itch. Oh, no. Now is not the time to sneeze. Not the time to sneeze . . .

Achoo! I sneeze.

"Bless you," says a Winkie. "I mean, curse you." Then he adds, "And just what do you think you're doing here?"

Oh, no! My sneeze gave us away. I'm out of ideas so I'm going to try honesty.

"The Wicked Witch of the West had her Winged Monkeys kidnap our friends!" I say, turning around. "They're just kids! Can you help us find them?" I ask.

The Winkie tilts his head. "Does one have brown hair in two braids and a blue-and-white dress?"

102

"Yes!" I cry. "That's Dorothy!"

"And does the other have reddish hair, a blue dress, and a green sweatshirt?"

"Yes! That's Robin," Frankie says.

"Don't know them," the Winkie says.

"Huh? You just described them!" Frankie cries.

"I've seen them," he says. "But I don't *know* them."

"Can you just show us where they are? So we can find them?" I ask. This conversation is getting ridiculous.

"No can do," the Winkie responds.

"And why not?" I demand.

"Because your friends aren't here," he explains.

"Is this one of those trick answers?" Frankie asks.

"Nope," the Winkie says. "You just missed them. The monkeys took them to the Emerald City about five minutes ago."

"What? Why?" I ask.

"Well, the witches have been trying to overpower the Wizard for years. And now that they've partnered up with that fairy guy — Gluck? Muck? — they are going to try to take the Wizard down! And then they'll conquer the Emerald City and turn it gray, too."

My stomach drops. So not only have we ruined the book and the movie, but now we might ruin the Emerald City for good?

Great. Just great.

"But why did the witches take Dorothy and Robin there?" I wonder out loud. "Couldn't they have just left them here in a dungeon or something?"

"It was that evil fairy," the Winkie says. "Gluck-Muck insisted your friends come along, too."

"Then we have to go to the Emerald City," I say.

"So we're off to see the Wizard?" Frankie asks.

"No," I say. "We're off to *save* the Wizard."

chapter ten

King of the Beasts

*t*he Winkies are nice enough to make us a pepperoni pizza before we go.

"The witches love pizza," one Winkie tells us, handing me the pizza in a take-out box. "They eat it for breakfast, lunch, and dinner. It's their favorite thing to eat, so we've become experts at making it. They like mice and frog legs as their toppings, though."

Frankie shudders. "Domino's definitely doesn't offer that on their menu."

Frankie and I leave the castle grounds and meet up with Penny, Toto, Prince, Scarecrow, and Tin Man, who have all been waiting eagerly for us. As soon as Prince sees me, he jumps up on his hind legs and his tail starts wagging. Aw, he really loves me.

Or maybe he just smells the pizza.

All seven of us sit down on the gray grass for a very quick pizza picnic. Scarecrow and Tin Man don't need food, so they just relax while the rest of us gobble up the delicious slices and gulp down the juice boxes the Winkies also sent us off with. When we're done eating and drinking, even Toto looks happier. Maybe he was just hangry.

Maybe that's Frankie's issue, too?

"Are you feeling better, Frankie?" I ask.

"What is that supposed to mean?" she snaps back.

Um, never mind.

"She seems fine to me," Tin Man says.

"Exactly," Frankie says. "He gets me. I'm just fine."

Whatever you say.

We throw away the remains of our picnic, and then we head back through the forest. We're on the lookout for the yellow brick road, which will take us to the Emerald City. The sun is starting to rise.

I yawn. After all that food, I could really use a nap. And some cold medicine. My nose is *really* stuffy.

Suddenly, something huge and furry and tan jumps right out at me.

"ROAR!"

"Ahhh!" we all shriek.

A ten-foot-tall lion is standing in front of us. Yes, standing. He's snarling, too, and pointing his sharp claws right at us.

"Lion!" Penny screams, stepping behind Tin Man with Toto in her arms. Toto whimpers and tries to escape.

Prince, ears flattened in fear, cowers behind Scarecrow.

"ROAR!" the Lion growls again, beating his white furry chest. "Roar!"

Everyone screams again.

But then I try to calm myself down.

107

"Guys, it's just the Cowardly Lion!" I say. "There's no reason to freak out!"

Lion's eyes flash. "Who are you calling cowardly?" he roars, looming over us. "I'll eat you for breakfast! ROAR! ROAR!"

Prince starts shaking beside me.

I've had enough. ENOUGH.

"No!" I yell. "No, no, no. Don't you try and scare us! I do not have the time for this! I am tired! I have a cold!"

"I knew you were sick," Penny says.

"Two of our friends have been kidnapped, we lost the magic shoes, the Emerald City has been taken over by witches, and it's up to us to save everyone. I do not have the patience to listen to you being a jerk!"

Lion stares at me. Then his face crumples. He bursts into tears!

"Waah!" he cries, tears streaming down his furry tan cheeks. "Waaaah!"

Seriously?

"Um, Mr. Lion?" I say. "Are you okay?"

He slashes his paws under his eyes to wipe tears away. "Why would I be okay? You just yelled at me. I'm very sensitive."

"No kidding," Penny says.

He hangs his head. "Are you going to yell at me for being sensitive?"

"No," I say calmly. "I'm sorry I yelled. But it's been a long night. We're in a bit of a jam."

Tin Man rubs his tin chin. "Mr. Lion," he begins. "Can I ask you something?"

"Sure," Lion says, plucking a leaf off a tree and blowing his nose into it.

"I thought lions were supposed to be kings of the jungle. Are you a different kind of lion?"

"Yeah," he says, hanging his head. "A cowardly one. The girl in the stained shirt is right."

"Told you," Penny says to me. "Totally stained."

I roll my eyes. Moving on.

"I'm a phony," Lion explains. "I know it, and now you

know it, too." He goes over to a fallen log and sits down and hangs his head.

"I know how you can prove you're not a scaredy-cat," Penny says. "Come with us to the Emerald City to fight the witches and evil fairy!"

Lion blanches. "Are you kidding me? I'm not fighting any witches or evil fairies! Why would I do that?"

"To help us save our friends," I say.

"And there's a reward for you, too," Penny says. "If you help us, I bet the Wizard will be so grateful that you helped that he'll give you some courage!"

"Really?" Lion asks.

"Penny!" I say, shaking my head. "The Wizard doesn't really have any magical powers. He's a fake. He's just a regular guy."

"That's not the way I remember it," she says. "In the movie he hands out courage to the Lion, a heart to the Tin Man, and a brain to the Scarecrow!"

Scarecrow throws his arms in the air. "So it's true? I can't wait to get a brain!"

"With all my heart," Tin Man says. "I would like a heart."

Frankie and I exchange glances. The Wizard is going to be a huge disappointment. But what can we say?

Lion nods. "I've thought it over. I'll join your team!"

"That's very brave of you!" Penny says.

Lion puffs up his chest. "It is? It is! See, it's working already!"

chapter eleven

Coffee, Please

Iion claims to know the way. "Follow me!" he says proudly, and goes racing down the dirt path through the forest.

"Wait for us! Not everyone is as fast as you!" Penny calls out. She is still holding Toto in her arms.

"Oops, sorry!" Lion says, slowing his pace to almost slow motion.

Finally, I see a clearing. And then something yellow glinting in the sun.

The yellow brick road! We're back.

"Follow the yellow brick road!" I cry. We're coming for you, Robin and Dorothy!

The sun is up, we're following the yellow brick road, and we're on our way to save our friends. I can't help but smile. Maybe I'm not feeling my healthiest, but I am turning this day around. And look at those beautiful red flowers!

"Ooh!" Penny exclaims, pointing at the flowers. "Pretty!"

"They are pretty!" Frankie says, looking around. For the first time in the past two days, she's smiling.

"I can give these to the Wizard," Scarecrow says. "That would be nice, right?" He takes a deep whiff of the flowers. "Ah, smells so lovely!"

I wish I could smell, but my nose is completely stuffed.

Toto and Prince are sniffing the flowers, too, leaping around and chasing each other. At least they seem to be getting along.

Wait. Wasn't there something important about red flowers in the movie?

What was it?

"Frankie?" I ask. "Aren't there red flowers in the story?"

Frankie looks up at me, in mid-sniff. Her eyes widen. She looks at the flowers in her hands. "Oh, no. They're poppies. They'll put us to sleep!"

Right! Oh, no.

"Penny! Lion! Scarecrow!" I cry. "Stop smelling the flowers!"

"Oh, stop being such a bossypants!" Penny calls over her shoulder.

"But the flowers are gonna put everyone to sleep!" I cry. "We don't have time to sleep! We have to beat the witches to the Emerald City!"

"It's worse than that," Frankie says, dropping her flowers like hot potatoes. "This is the kind of sleep where we might never wake up. We have to get away from the flowers as soon as we . . ." She sways, and blinks. "I'm soooo tired."

"Why are my eyes so heavy?" Lion asks, also swaying. "I'm getting sleepy. Can someone make me a cup of coffee? No, a *pot* of coffee? A swimming pool of coffee?" Without any warning, he face-plants onto the field.

Prince scurries away just in time to avoid getting hit by the falling lion.

Frankie sinks to the ground, and within seconds she is snoring away.

"Oh, no!" I cry.

Penny drops next, also snoring happily.

"What's wrong with them?" Tin Man asks.

"The flowers are putting them to sleep!" I say. "No!" I cry to my friends. No, no, no! "Stay awake! People, you need to stay awake! We have to get to the Emerald City! Where's Prince? Toto?"

I look around and spot both dogs curled into little napping balls beside Penny.

Am I going to fall asleep next? Why am I still awake? I look at Tin Man and Scarecrow. We're standing while Lion, the two dogs, Frankie, and Penny all sleep.

"I don't understand what's happening," Scarecrow says. "Are we supposed to be taking naps now?"

"No, we're not!" I say. "They just walked into a field of poppies and fell asleep!"

"But why aren't *we* asleep?" Scarecrow asks.

"Maybe because we're not humans or animals?" Tin Man asks. "Abby, are you a human?"

"I am definitely a human," I reply. And then I sneeze. "But my nose is stuffed, so maybe that stopped me from breathing in the scent of the poppies?"

"Well, what do we do now?" Scarecrow asks. "How long do you think they will sleep for?"

I rack my brain to try and remember what happened in the movie. All of them fell asleep . . . but then Glinda the good witch made it snow on them, which woke them up!

"Glinda!" I cry to the sky. "Help us! Make it snow!"

I wait. And wait. I don't see Glinda. Or snow.

"Who's Glinda?" Tin Man asks.

"Ugh," I say. "She's a good witch. Although apparently not a very reliable one."

"There's a good witch?" Scarecrow asks.

"There's supposed to be," I grumble. "But this one has

been missing in action." It's not totally her fault. I remember what Frankie said — in the book, Glinda comes to help because the Munchkins get her. So in *this* version Glinda doesn't even know about us yet. Understandable, but what do we do now? This is so unfair. I'm the one who's sick and needs to nap, yet my friends are the ones who get to sleep while I have to figure out how to save everyone!

"Maybe we should move them away from the flowers?" Tin Man asks. "So they're not breathing the air in?"

I nod. "That makes sense," I say.

"You're really smart, Tin Man," Scarecrow says. "I can't wait to get my brain from the Wizard."

He looks so wistful, I don't have the heart to remind him that the Wizard is a big fake. I sneeze again and try really hard not to breathe in.

"And when I get my heart," Tin Man says, "no one will be happier for you than me!"

And I'll just be happy when my friends wake up so we can

rescue Robin and Dorothy. I hope they're okay. And not too scared.

"Tin Man, you grab Penny," I say. "Scarecrow, you take Frankie. I'll take the dogs. Then we'll come back for Lion. He's so big we'll have to work together to get him out of the field. I'll try to keep breathing out of my mouth, but if I fall asleep, you need to move me, too!"

I scoop both dogs into my arms and run with them to the end of the field. I set them down beside a tree.

Tin Man carries Penny. Scarecrow carries Frankie. Once both girls are next to the dogs, all three of us rush back in for Lion.

SNORE-zzzzz! comes out of Lion, his furry white belly rising up and down. *Zzzzz-SNORE!*

"Wow, that's loud," Tin Man says. "And he has terrible breath. He could really brush his teeth occasionally."

"Scarecrow," I say, "you take Lion's head. Tin Man, you take his body. I'll hold up his feet."

Together, we finally move Lion over by the girls.

The three of us sit down, exhausted.

Everyone's still asleep.

"Come on, all," I say. "Wake up!"

"Yawwwwwwwn!"

That wasn't me. Or Scarecrow. Or Tin Man. I look over at my friends. Frankie is stretching her arms over her head, her mouth in a big yawn.

Yes! She's waking up!

"I can't believe I forgot about the poppies," she says, and straightens her glasses.

Penny stretches and yawns, too, her blue eyes popping open. "Why is there a twig in my hair?" she complains, yanking it out.

Lion is still snoring away.

"What happened?" Penny asks.

"Remember the poppy scene in the movie?" I ask. "We just went through it."

"Oops," she says. "We all fell asleep?"

"I didn't," I say.

"Because you have a cold! I knew it!" she exclaims once again.

"Yes," I say. "I have a cold. A thousand apologies."

"If you get me sick, you are not forgiven," she says.

Frankie stands up. "Let's go. We've wasted enough time." She pokes Lion in the paw. "Wake up already!"

"Whoa," I say. "We moved him last. It might take him a few more minutes to snap out of his trance."

Lion opens one eye. "Roar?"

"Time to get up," Frankie says.

Toto licks Lion's cheek. Aw.

Penny giggles.

Lion stretches himself in a sun salutation.

"Okay, everyone," I say. "Now that you've all had your beauty sleep, it's time to get moving again. Lion, do you know how much longer we have to walk to get to the Emerald City?"

"Maybe about twenty minutes. Make that forty for you slowpokes."

"How will we know when we're there?" Scarecrow asks.

"We'll know," Lion says.

Eventually we see it.

A shiny green wall.

The city must be on the other side of it.

"Yay, we made it!" I say. "We've arrived at the gates of the Emerald City!"

"Now what?" Lion asks. "Do you think the witches are already here?"

Everyone stops to think.

"We can just ring the bell," Tin Man says. He points to the buzzer on the gate with a sign. PRESS TO REQUEST ENTRY.

"But if we ring it and they *are* here, then they'll know *we're* here," I say. "I don't think we want the witches and Gluck to know."

"Good point," Frankie says.

"Maybe we shouldn't even be here," Penny says, looking scared. "Two witches, an evil fairy, and flying monkeys? Can't we just go home?"

"We need to get the shoes to go home," I explain. "And we can't leave Robin! Or Dorothy!"

"Right," Penny grumbles. "Why did Robin have to get herself snatched up?"

"It's not her fault!" I say. "Robin didn't even know the flying monkeys existed!"

"Can you guys stop fighting?" Frankie asks. "You're getting on my nerves!"

"*You're* getting on *my* nerves," Penny says. "You've been on my nerves all day, Cranky Frankie!"

"Stop calling me that!" Frankie cries.

"Pssst," I hear.

What was that?

I see a small gray face peer at me from between two of the slabs in the gate.

"Hi," I say, startled. "Who are you?"

"I'm the Gate Guard," the gray woman says. "Who are *you*?"

"I'm Abby, and this is Penny, Frankie, Toto, Prince,

Scarecrow, Tin Man, and Lion. We're looking for our friends," I say.

"You do not want to be inside the Emerald City," the gray woman says. "We've been taken over by witches and an evil fairy!"

"Oh, no," I say. "They're here already?"

She nods. "The three of them flew in and took over the whole city!"

"Where's the Wizard?"

"He barricaded himself in the throne room in his castle!"

Such a wimp, that wizard.

"And did they fly in with any prisoners?" I ask.

"Yes! Two young girls."

"Where are they?" I ask. "We need to rescue them!"

"I'll only tell you if you promise to overthrow the witches and the evil fairy so Oz can be ours again. Will you help us?"

I look at the rest of our crew.

The dogs bark and jump in circles. Everyone else nods.

"It's a deal," I say.

chapter twelve

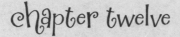

The Not-So-Emerald City

*t*he gate to the Emerald City creaks open slowly, and we all step inside.

Clank! The gate instantly closes, locking us in.

I jump. So does Penny.

Wait. A. Minute. Penny is gray. All gray. Skin. Hair. Clothes!

Prince's fur is no longer brown and white! He's turned gray, too. And so has Toto. And Scarecrow. And Tin Man. *And* Lion.

Ahhh!

"Abby, you're gray!" Penny cries.

We look at one another. All of us are gloomy gray!

"What's wrong with us?" I ask the gray woman who let us through the gate.

"The witches cast a spell on the Emerald City, turning everything inside gray," she explains.

"But it's the Emerald City!" Penny says. "It's supposed to be green!"

"Actually," Frankie says, "in the book, the Wizard makes everyone wear emerald glasses so that everything *looks* green. But the city is no greener than any other city. Only the outside wall is really green."

"I'd rather look green than gray," Penny says, frowning at her gray arms. "Gray is so depressing. We look like we're in a newspaper."

I take in the scene around me. It does kind of look like we're in a newspaper. Everything is various shades of gray. The people. Buildings. Shops.

"Hey, you're all the same color as me now!" Tin Man says.

Penny looks him over. "You're normally much more silver than gray. It wouldn't be as bad if we were metallic toned. Hey, do you think we can still get makeovers?"

"Huh?" I say. "What makeovers? What are you talking about?"

"Didn't you see the movie?" Penny asks. "When Dorothy goes to the Emerald City she gets her hair and her nails done! At the same time! It's my favorite scene in the whole movie."

Frankie snorts. "That doesn't happen in the book."

"It doesn't?" Penny cries. "But that's why I wanted to come to the Emerald City! Are you telling me I'm risking my life with the Winged Monkeys and I'm not even getting a makeover?"

"You should have just gone to a spa in Smithville," Frankie snaps.

What is up with her? "Frankie, is everything okay?" I ask.

"No!" she replies sharply. "It's not! And I don't want to talk about it!"

Ouch. Okay, then.

We're all quiet.

Tin Man speaks up. "I wonder if they should change the name of this place from the Emerald City to the Gray City. Or the Concrete City?" He's clearly trying to change the subject.

"Hide!" the guardian yells suddenly. "They're flying over us!"

We look up to see two figures on broomsticks zoom right through the gray sky. They fly by so fast, I can barely make them out. Just a blur of black, white, and gray. But I think I recognize one of them as the Wicked Witch of the East; the other must be her sister.

They're trailed by a crew of flying monkeys. The flying monkey in front has Gluck's face.

We all press ourselves against the wall, trying to be as inconspicuous as possible.

"Where are the witches going?" I ask the guardian.

"Breakfast," she says.

"Pizza, right?" I ask.

The guardian nods. "They really like pizza," she says.

"Who doesn't," I say. "What kind of toppings did they get?"

"Spiders and frogs," she says. "Also, butterflies."

Ew.

"But yes, on their schedule today is breakfast, and then they called a mandatory city-wide meeting for high noon in the town square."

"Why?" I ask.

"To scare us, I suppose," she says. "And boss us around."

"We need to help our friends escape," I say. "Can you tell us where they are?"

"They're in Tigertail Tower," she says. "But you'll need the Wizard's help to get in there. Trust me. And then together, all your magic combined will overtake the witches!"

"What magic?" Frankie asks. "We don't have any magic."

She peers at us. "You're not a fairy? Or a witch?"

"Nope," Penny says.

The guardian frowns. "You have no magic powers at all? What are you?"

"Just kids," I say. "And two dogs. And a lion, a scarecrow, and a tin man. They can talk. Is that considered magical?"

"Is that all they can do?"

"I'm a pretty good dancer," Lion says. "Do you want to see me Floss?"

"No," she says, frowning. "Flossing will not help you save your friends and defeat the witches!" She is clearly exasperated.

"I can do the Macarena," Tin Man adds.

The guardian sighs and shakes her head. "Save the Wizard first. Then get your friends. Then you can practice your dance moves."

"We're hoping the Wizard can help us anyway," Lion says. "I could use some courage, my tin friend could use a heart, and my straw friend could use a brain."

Frankie rolls her eyes. "He can't do any of that."

"You never know," Penny says.

"We know," Frankie says.

"He can help you," the woman tells Lion. "He's the great and powerful Wizard of Oz."

"So powerful he barricaded himself in his room?" Frankie asks.

"He's no match for two witches *and* an evil fairy!" she cries.

"Speaking of our favorite evil fairy," I say, "where *is* Gluck? We have to keep an eye out for him, too. Remember that he can transform."

"He could be anyone?" Frankie says.

I nod. "Anyone or anything. Let's be on high alert," I say.

We thank the guardian and rush over to the castle to find the Wizard. We get a bunch of strange looks as we go. It's hard to blend in when you're with a ten-foot lion, a scarecrow whose legs keep wobbling, and a tin man who creaks with every step.

"Hurry," I whisper. "Keep your eyes down and walk as fast as you can."

A gray man in a gray uniform and gray top hat is standing in front of the castle.

"I guess that's the castle guard," I say.

"I could roar really loudly and scare him away," Lion suggests.

"That might call attention to us," I say. "We don't want the witches or Gluck to know we're here."

Just then, I spot the Winged Monkeys overhead, flying lower then before.

"No, no, no, no, no, no," cries Penny, her shoulders shaking.

"We have to get inside!" I call out. "They're going to see us!"

"Go, go, I'll distract the guard," Tin Man says. "He might officially work for the witches but . . ."

"No one who works for the witches actually likes the witches," I say, thinking of Orly and the Winkies.

"Right," Tin Man says. "He's probably not that loyal. You sneak in. Then I'll find you."

While Tin Man walks up to the gray guard, we quickly sneak past the big gray trees to a side door. I pull the handle.

"Locked!" I mutter.

"I can pull that door off its hinges with a pinkie," Lion says. He grabs the door handle and gives it a yank, and it opens.

"Yay!" I say. "Thanks, Lion!"

He smiles proudly.

We all rush in. There is a long dark hallway in front of us. Frankie, Prince, Scarecrow, and I start marching forward.

But Lion doesn't move. And neither does Penny. They're both still at the front door.

"Hey," I whisper. "Something wrong?"

Lion's front paws are trembling. His now-gray nose is quivering.

Penny's hands are doing the same. And she has Toto in her arms.

"I'm scared," Lion says.

"Me too," says Penny. Her voice is shaking. "We don't know what's at the end of the hall."

"There's nothing at the end of the hall," Frankie says. "The Wizard has no powers. The only thing we have to fear is fear itself."

"Is that in the book?" Penny asks.

"No," Frankie says. "Franklin Delano Roosevelt said it. He was the president a long time ago."

"That sounds so wise," Scarecrow says.

Penny shakes her head. "There is *something* to fear, though. What if there is something scary at the end of the hall?"

"Maybe don't worry about what's at the end of the hall just yet," Scarecrow says. "Just worry about taking that first step. Then you can worry about taking the next step. One step at a time."

Wow! *Scarecrow* is so wise!

"We can do one step at a time," Penny says. She nuzzles

her chin against Toto. "Right, Toto? Right, Lion?"

Lion puts his paw around Penny's shoulders. "Right."

"I'll walk beside you two," Tin Man says, sneaking inside. "Just in case you need a pep talk."

Aw. Penny and Lion are being brave! And it seems to me that Scarecrow is pretty smart and Tin Man might have a big heart already.

I scoop up Prince and we all head down the hall and into the blackness together.

"We got this," I say.

At the end of the hall is a massive black throne.

And suddenly, a huge black-and-white head appears above it! The head is bigger than my whole body. I gasp and Penny shrieks.

"Who dares enter my private throne room?" the head demands.

"It's not real," I say. "Remember it's not real!"

"It may not be real, but it's real scary," Penny says, her voice wobbling.

We all take a step back.

"You dare to try to overtake the Emerald City?" the head booms. "You will fail!"

"No," I say. "Mr. Wizard, we're not —"

"Silence!" the Wizard bellows. "You're making me angry. And do you know what happens when I get angry?"

"Wh-what?" Lion asks nervously.

"This!" the Wizard booms, and black fire erupts all around him, the flames crackling.

My eyes widen. Prince is trembling in my arms. Penny is shaking and clutching Toto against her. Lion is cowering. Even Scarecrow is shaking now, since he's probably worried about what happens to fire and straw. And Tin Man is trembling, too.

I know this is all fake, but it sure seems real.

"Enough!" Frankie yells. She's the only one of us not shaking. She marches right over to the fire, walks right through the head, and yanks away a curtain that I hadn't noticed before.

And suddenly, standing there is a short man with a regular-sized bald head. Behind him is a film projector and an electric fireplace that's shooting up flames.

We all gasp.

"Ahhh!" the Wizard shrieks.

"What happened to your giant head?" the Lion asks.

"It was all fake!" Frankie says. "He was doing that with the projector and the electric fireplace! He's not a real wizard! How many times do I have to tell everyone?"

The Wizard hangs his head. "She's right. I'm not a real wizard. I'm a fraud with no powers at all. I'm just a regular guy. My name is Bob."

"So you can't give me courage?" Lion asks.

"And you can't give me a brain?" Scarecrow asks.

"No heart?" asks Tin Man.

He shakes his head. "I can't."

We all just stand there.

"Can you help save our other friends?" I ask.

He cocks his head to the side. "I don't know. Does it involve magic?"

"Magic wouldn't hurt," I say. "But somehow, we need to get them out of Tigertail Tower."

"Would the key help?" he asks.

I laugh. "Yes," I say. "Yes, it would."

chapter thirteen

Escape from the Tower

*t*he Wizard, aka Bob, fishes a golden key out of a drawer beside the projector. "Here you go," he says. "Good luck!"

"You're not coming?" I ask, incredulous. "You need to show us where the tower is!"

Bob shakes his head. "It's far. And I'd have to walk across the city. See, I never leave the castle. If I go out, everyone will realize the truth about me. And anyway, if anyone saw me outside I'd be mobbed and your cover would be blown. You're trying to be sneaky, right?"

"I guess," I say.

"Just go straight down Salty Street, turn right on Blue Avenue, and then left on Purple Lane. Then just cross the bridge, and voilà, you're there."

I hand Prince over to Penny, who takes him in her free arm. "Will you watch him while I'm gone?" I ask. Penny nods. "I'll be right back," I whisper to Prince.

"I'll come with you, Abby!" Tin Man calls out.

"Is that a good idea?" Scarecrow asks. "You're kind of creaky. You don't want the monkeys to hear you."

"Well, *you're* kind of wobbly! You can barely stand on your own," Tin Man snaps.

"I'm too tall and furry," Lion says. "I should definitely wait here for you all. I shouldn't leave the castle. Nope."

"Maybe it's best if only two people go," Frankie says. "So we don't get caught. I can go. I'm assuming Penny is too scared anyway."

Penny turns red and cuddles Toto and Prince closer to her.

"Frankie," I say under my breath. "You don't have to be mean about it."

"I'm being honest!" she says. "Is it mean to be honest?"

"You're the one who needs a heart," Penny mutters.

"You're the one who needs some courage," Frankie says to her.

I turn to Frankie. "What is up with you today? You really are being mean!"

She narrows her eyes. "If I'm so mean, go on your own! You got us into this mess with your weird fairy tale mirror. You can get us out of it!"

I feel like she slapped me across the face. "Okay," I sputter.

"Make sure Dorothy has the shoes so we can actually go home," Frankie adds.

"Anything else?" I ask, narrowing my eyes.

"That's it," she says.

I kiss Prince good-bye, then storm out of the castle through the front door.

*   *   *

I'm about halfway across the Emerald (now Gray) City when I hear someone calling behind me.

"Abby, wait!"

I turn around. It's Frankie.

"What?" I ask.

"I'll come with you," she says.

She will? "Are you still going to be mean?" I ask.

"Was I being mean?" she asks with a shrug.

"Yes!"

She shrugs again. "Sorry. Let's go to Tigertail Tower."

Okay, fine. But I hope she doesn't think I'm forgiving her with that half-baked apology.

We sneak through the city, trying to be casual. I smile self-consciously at the gray people and keep an eye out for the witches. They must still be eating breakfast. After walking along a cobblestoned street, we cross the small bridge over the moat to where the tower is.

There is no guard in front of it. But the door is locked.

141

I take the gold key out of my pocket and put it inside the lock. Please let this work, please let this work . . . it works!

The lock clicks and the door opens.

"Hurrah!" I say.

Inside, there's a steep, winding staircase that leads to a metal door a few stories up.

"Maybe I'll go up and let them out?" I offer to Frankie. "You can stay here in case something goes wrong," I suggest.

"Sure," she says.

I climb up the stairs quickly, trying not to lose my breath. I knock softly on the door. "Guys? You in there?"

"Abby! Is that you?" It's Robin's voice. I feel a rush of relief.

"Yes!" I say. "I'm here to rescue you!"

"Thank goodness!"

I take the gold key out of my pocket again, put it in the lock, and . . . please let this work again, please let this work again . . . it turns! It works! Yes!

I push the door open. Dorothy and Robin are waiting eagerly on the other side.

Robin throws her arms around me. "You saved us!"

"I'm so glad I found you," I say, hugging Robin back. I even give Dorothy a hug.

"Thank you!" Dorothy cries. "Where is Toto? Is he okay?"

"He's fine," I assure her. "He's back at the Wizard's castle with Penny and Prince." I study Dorothy and Robin; they're both gray, of course, but otherwise they don't seem harmed. "What happened to you two?" I ask.

Robin groans. "It was awful. The flying monkeys carried us across Oz, and first we went to the witch's castle. But then we left *again* and the flying monkeys dumped us in this tower and locked the door. We've been stuck here ever since."

"I'm sorry," I say.

"It gets worse," Dorothy says. "The witches took the magic shoes!"

I glance down and see with horror that Dorothy is barefoot. Noooo.

"I was trying to figure out how Dorothy should use them," Robin explains. "But then the witches swooped in and grabbed them from us." She sighs. "So I had no idea what to do! I didn't know the story! I wish I had seen the movie! Why did I never see the movie?" She slaps her forehead.

"It's an old movie," I tell her, and although I am bummed about the magic shoes, I add, "And we'll figure out what to do about the shoes."

"Still! I just felt so dumb. So so so dumb! Dorothy kept asking me what was going to happen and I had no idea."

"It's not your fault," I tell her. "It's just a movie. And a book, but I haven't read the book, either. You're not dumb."

"I felt dumb," Robin says. "I still do. I don't even understand where we are."

"We're in the Emerald City," I say.

"But why is it called that when everything in it is gray?" She throws her hands up. "It makes no sense!"

"Well, see, it's because of the witches —" I say.

"Can I go find Toto?" Dorothy asks, interrupting us. "I miss my little pup."

"Yes!" I'm missing Prince, too. I turn back toward the door. "The staircase is narrow, so be careful."

I wave to Frankie, who's at the foot of the stairs. "Got 'em!" I tell her.

She waves. "I wouldn't take them on the staircase," she tells me.

"Huh?" I ask. "Why not? Is there another way down?"

"Nope!" she says gleefully.

"Then why?" I ask.

She lifts her right hand. She's holding a wand of some sort. "Because it's gone!" She twirls her hand, and the next thing I know the staircase has disappeared.

I step back before I fall. "What just happened?"

"I trapped you!" she exclaims.

"Why would you do that, Frankie?" Robin asks.

"Isn't she your friend?" Dorothy asks.

A cold realization creeps over my body. "No," I say. "She's not. It's not Frankie."

The girl who looks like Frankie snaps her fingers, and suddenly, Gluck is standing at the bottom of the tower.

"You're right!" he cackles. "I'm not! Frankie never followed you! I did! And now your other friends are locked inside the Wizard's castle, and you're stuck up there . . . forever! You'll never be able to help Maryrose from here. And just in case you even think of jumping . . ." He flicks his wand again, and a massive tiger appears beside him.

Oh. No.

"A tiger for Tigertail Tower!" he exclaims, laughing. "Okay," he says, and checks his watch. "I have to get back to my own world now. There's a big evil fairy party that I do *not* want to miss. But I don't think you're going anywhere. So bye! Enjoy Oz! Guess you'll never be freeing Maryrose!"

He flicks his wand one last time and disappears.

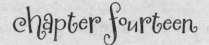

chapter fourteen

Stuck

this is bad.

Frankie/Gluck is gone, and Robin, Dorothy, and I are stuck at the top of a tower, at least thirty feet off the concrete ground. Way too far to jump without seriously injuring ourselves.

And also there is a tiger at the bottom. A tiger!

"I'm never going back to Kansas, am I?" Dorothy asks, her eyes filling with tears.

I take a deep breath. "We're getting you home. I promise."

I look out the open door that leads to nothing. Now *my* eyes prick with tears. I need to fix this! But what am I going to do?

I notice that the tiger below has curled up and is taking a nap. Well, that's promising. But it's still way too far for Robin, Dorothy, and me to jump down.

"Abby, look," Robin says. "There's a lion downstairs!"

"It's a tiger," I tell her. "Gluck zapped up a tiger."

"I know," she says. "But now there's a lion, too."

Huh?

I look down and see that there is indeed a lion. And not just any lion. Our Lion!

Aww!

Just then, Penny, Toto, Prince, Scarecrow, Tin Man, Bob, and Frankie sneak in beside Lion. Is Frankie the real Frankie? I peer closely at her. I hope so.

The tiger starts to stir.

Oh, no.

Lion looks like he's about to turn around and run, but

Penny tells him, "You can do this! You're the king of the forest!"

Lion nods to himself, throws his shoulders back, and lets out a massive roar.

The tiger growls back.

"Roar!"

"Growl!"

"Roaaaaar!"

"Groooooowl."

"Roar!"

"Growl?"

Suddenly, they both start laughing.

"Um, what's so funny?" Frankie asks.

Lion smiles. "Turns out the tiger knows my little sister. What a small world, huh?"

Omg. Lion and the tiger were *talking*! Well, first they were probably fighting, but then it turned into talking.

"Don't worry, she won't hurt us," Lion adds.

Thank goodness. I exhale in relief.

Prince and Toto start barking at each other. Are they talking, too?

"Lions and tigers and dogs, oh, my," Dorothy says.

I carefully lean over the side. "How did you get out?" I ask everyone standing below.

"The Gluck fairy locked us inside the Wizard's castle, but he didn't know about the underground tunnels," Penny says.

"Only I knew about those," Bob says.

"So here we are!" Tin Man says.

I look down at them all and then focus on Frankie. "Wait a sec. How do I know you're the real Frankie?" I ask. "Gluck pretended to be you before."

Her jaw drops. "He did?"

I nod. "He caught up to me and apologized. Then when I climbed up here he made the stairs disappear!"

"Oh, no!" she says. "I can't believe he did that! But I'm really me, I swear."

Lion narrows his eyes at her and studies her suspiciously. "How can we tell if it's really her?"

Frankie looks up at me. "You have to trust me."

"If you want us to trust you, can you tell us why you've been so mean all day?" Penny asks her.

Yeah. Why?

Frankie looks at all of us. "I wasn't really planning on talking about this at all, never mind in front of, um, all the *Wizard of Oz* characters, right in the middle of an attempted tower escape . . ."

"The timing isn't great," Tin Man agrees.

". . . but you're right," Frankie goes on. "I know I've been cranky. It's not about you guys at all. See . . . my dad has to go to Europe for his job for six months. And I'm really going to miss him. I'm sorry if I've been taking my stress out on all of you. When it's not your fault."

"Oh, Frankie," I say, stepping closer but not too close to the edge. "You should have told us!"

"I know," she says, looking up. "I just . . . It made me sad to talk about."

"Frankie, we love you and we're here for you whenever you want to talk," Robin says.

"Yes," I say. "Exactly."

"Can we get back to the rescue here?" Dorothy asks. "And maybe talk this out at a later time?"

"It's not all about you, Dorothy!" Penny calls up, and turns to Frankie. "I'm sorry I called you heartless."

"I'm sorry I called you a coward," Frankie says to Penny. "Especially since coming to save Abby was your idea."

"It was?" I ask.

Penny nods. "It totally was." She beams. "Look at me, all brave!"

I nod. "Okay," I say. "So . . . back to the rescue. You snuck in! Together! Amazing! What's part two of the plan?"

We stare down. They stare up.

"Do you want to jump and we'll catch you?" Lion asks.

I look down at the concrete floor. "Not particularly."

Robin turns to me. "What if they make a ladder?"

"Out of wood?" I ask.

"No," she says. "Out of them. A human ladder. Or more

accurately, a human, animal, scarecrow, and tin ladder? They should be able to reach us and then we won't have to jump."

"We could do that," Scarecrow says. "Good thinking!"

"Thank you," Robin says, flushing with pride.

"See?" I say. "Smart!"

She smiles. "Maybe."

"I'm scared of heights," Lion says sheepishly. "But I can definitely be on the bottom!"

"I'll be next," Tin Man says. "Because no weight can crush me."

"Growl!" says the tiger.

"She'll go on top of Tin Man," Lion says.

"I'm not great with heights," Penny says. "Maybe I can direct?"

Frankie raises an eyebrow.

"Fine, I'll get in there," she grumbles. "We better not fall."

Lion crouches down and Tin Man gets on top of his shoulders. Then the tiger climbs on top and then Bob the Wizard goes next. Then Scarecrow. Then Lion holds out his leg. Penny steps onto it. Tin Man holds out his hand. She continues up the ladder with the help of the others. Then Scarecrow puts out his hand and pulls her right up on his shoulders.

"I got this," she says. "I got this!"

Frankie does the same. And suddenly, Frankie is right under me!

"Hi," I say, waving. "Dorothy, you go first, 'kay?"

Dorothy hesitates, but then Frankie leads her into her arms.

"Got you!" Frankie says.

On the ground, Toto barks happily.

Dorothy climbs all the way down and scoops her dog up. "I missed you so much, Toto," she says, burying her face in his fur.

"Aw, now *I* miss him," Penny says.

"Thanks for taking such good care of him," Dorothy says to Penny.

Penny, still on Scarecrow's shoulders, nods but looks a little sad.

Robin goes next.

And then, finally, me!

"Yes!" I exclaim when I touch the ground. "We did it!"

We all high-five, and Prince leaps into my arms.

Tigertail Tower is suddenly pretty crowded. There's me, Penny, Frankie, Robin, Dorothy, Scarecrow, Lion, Tin Man, Bob the Wizard, Toto, Prince, *plus* a random tiger. Who is now deep in conversation with Lion about other animals they know in common. Carnivore networking.

"We really have to go," I say.

"But how do we get home?" Frankie asks. "We don't have the shoes!"

Penny turns to Bob. "Can't you help us? Do you have any magical powers at all?"

He shakes his head. "I'm sorry," he says. "I'm a total fraud."

"So we need to get the shoes," I say. "It's our only way home."

"We got them once," Penny says. "We can get them again."

"But how?" Robin asks.

"It's not ideal," Frankie says. "Maybe we'll get lucky and it will rain on the witches."

"It never rains in Oz," Scarecrow says.

"Thank goodness!" Tin Man says, shivering. "Do you know how rusty I would be?"

"So what else can we do?" I ask.

"Wait," Scarecrow says to Bob. "You said you don't have magical powers, right?"

"Don't rub it in!" Bob groans.

Scarecrow shakes his head. "But do the witches know that? Don't *they* think you have magical powers?"

Bob nods. "They do. Everyone in Oz thinks I do."

Scarecrow's eyes brighten. "So can't we trick them?"

I feel a surge of hope. "Scarecrow!" I cry. "You're brilliant!"

He blushes. "I am?"

"Yes!" I say excitedly. "Here's what we do. We show up at their high-noon assembly and act like we are all-powerful.

We tell them we have weather magic and that we'll rain all over them if they don't hand over the shoes!" I say in a burst of inspiration.

"Are we all in, then?" Frankie asks.

Everyone nods.

"Let's do it," I say.

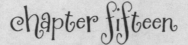

chapter fifteen

Bob Is Everywhere

All the inhabitants of the Emerald City are waiting in a circle in the town square. There are Winkies and Munchkins here, too. The witches must have brought them over from the other areas of Oz to help run the city.

I look over at the Munchkins. Is that Orly? It is! I wave to her and she super-subtly waves back. I'm glad she didn't get in trouble for helping us escape. The Winged Monkeys are here, too, flying overhead, keeping an eye on everyone. Our entire squad — Bob, Tin Man, Lion, Scarecrow, Frankie, Robin,

Penny, Dorothy, the two dogs, and I — are in position and trying to oh-so-casually wait for the witches. Our new tiger friend is here, too, just in case we need extra backup.

We came to the square a bit earlier to set up, carrying bags of the Wizard's disguises.

"Are you sure this is going to work?" Robin whispers to me.

"No," I say. "But I don't know what else to try! We need those shoes. And we promised we'd help free Emerald City from the witches!"

Suddenly, we hear them above.

Swoop! Swoop! Swoop!

The two witches zip through the sky on their brooms and land in the town square.

"Welcome to the Gray City!" the Wicked Witch of the East says with a laugh, throwing back her head. She's wearing a gray crown with gray stones, and she still has on Penny's checkered sneakers.

Her sister laughs, too, her cackle even more high-pitched.

She has on the same crown, but *she's* wearing the silver slippers. "We are now your new leaders!" she announces.

I glance up. The Winged Monkeys are flying in circles overhead. Ready to take away anyone who disagrees with the witches, I guess. I don't see any monkeys that have Gluck's face, but that doesn't mean he's not here.

"We want the Wizard!" Penny suddenly cries out from the crowd, just as we planned.

"Who said that?" the Wicked Witch of the West asks, peering into the crowd.

No one answers.

"The Wizard is a wimp!" shouts the Wicked Witch of the East. "As soon as we arrived he barricaded himself in his castle. He is hiding from us! He knows his magic is no match for ours!"

"She's right," Bob whispers to me, trembling. "It isn't! I'm a total fraud!"

"But they don't know that!" I remind him. "Ready?"

"Ready," he says nervously. Then he clears his throat,

stands up as tall as he can, and shouts, "I am not a wimp! I am the great and powerful Wizard of Oz!"

Except because he is a ventriloquist — he's able to throw his voice — it sounds like he's speaking from the *other* side of the crowd.

"Let us see you!" the Wicked Witch of the East calls out, spinning around to find him.

"I am everywhere and everything," the Wizard booms, his voice now coming from a *different* direction.

"Prove it!" the Wicked Witch of the West says.

From the other side of the crowd, the Wizard's giant head pops up. The head has no body — it's just a head. Well, technically, Frankie is holding up the head, but no one else can see that.

"I am the great and powerful Wizard of Oz!" the head says. "And I do not like being challenged!"

I can see the Wizard's mouth moving beside me — even though the voice sounds like it's coming from the head. The Wizard is really good at this voice-throwing thing.

The townspeople gasp.

The head disappears.

A massive ball of fire pops up on the other side of the circle. It's actually Tin Man holding up a huge cotton ball soaked in oil and set aflame. The Wizard's voice booms again: "I am ordering the Wicked Witch of the West and the Wicked Witch of the East to leave the Emerald City!"

The fire disappears, and then Lion, who is wearing a beast costume, rears up on his hind legs. He has the head of a rhinoceros with five eyes on its face, as well as five arms and five legs, and it is covered in fur. People in the crowd start screaming in fear.

"Leave now and I will let you live!" the Wizard roars, making it seem like the scary beast is speaking.

The witches both laugh. "You don't scare us!" the Wicked Witch of the West declares.

"I should," the Wizard says, his voice now coming from above somehow. "I am very magical! So magical! And I am not asking for much. I am asking for you to just leave us alone!"

"And the shoes," I whisper to him. "We need the shoes!"

"And the shoes," he adds. "We need the shoes!"

"Both pairs!" Penny cries out.

"No," the Wicked Witch of the West says.

"Definitively not," her sister adds.

The Wizard looks at me. "What now?" he whispers.

"Tell them you'll drop a house on them if they don't do what you say," I whisper.

"But I can't actually do that," he says.

"I know! But you have to scare them."

The Wizard nods, and shouts, "If you two don't listen to me, I will drop a house on you!"

The Wicked Witch of the West laughs again. "Two people already tried that yesterday, and it didn't work. What else do you got?"

"You'll make it rain," I whisper to the Wizard.

"I'll make it rain!" he says.

"Yeah?" the Wicked Witch of the East taunts. "Go ahead! Let's see you do that!"

Everyone waits.

The Wizard looks at me.

No raindrops fall from the gray sky.

"See?" the witch says. "You can't! You can't stop us! I bet you don't even have any magic at all!"

The crowd gasps.

The Wicked Witch of the West scans the crowd, and her gaze lands on me. I freeze.

"Ah, I see that the girl who tried to squash my sister is here!" the witch snarls. "She came to rescue you all, did she? Are her friends here, too? Monkeys, get me the girl and her friends!"

Oh, no!

Before we can run, the Winged Monkeys have us all by the collars! Eeeee! And up, up, up we go, high into the sky. My stomach drops and I look around at my friends in panic. Frankie, Penny, Robin, and Dorothy are all being carried up by the flying monkeys, too. I glance down at the crowd and search frantically for Prince, but I can't see him.

"Toto!" Dorothy cries, but she clearly can't see him from way up here, either.

Finally, the monkeys set us down right in front of the wicked witches. My friends and I huddle together as the witches glare at us.

"You five are revolting," the Wicked Witch of the East says. "We will lock you in my dungeon again, and this time you will rot there until the end of time."

The end of time sounds long.

And we definitely won't be back in Smithville for dinner.

Gluck did end up trapping us here, just like he wanted.

What can we do? How can we ever get out of this?

"I'm scared," Dorothy says, trembling.

"It'll be okay," Penny tells her.

"Does anyone have a pail of water?" Frankie calls out. "We could really use a pail of water about now! A bottle of water would be fine, too! A Dixie cup?"

No answer. Crumbs.

"Monkeys, take them away!" the Wicked Witch of the West cackles.

The monkeys are swooping down to pick us up again when Prince runs into the center of the circle.

"Prince, be careful!" I cry.

Grrr-rowl! he barks, running straight for the Wicked Witch of the East.

Gr-rowl! Toto barks in agreement, running right for the Wicked Witch of the West.

"Get away from us, you disgusting animals!" the Wicked Witch of the East snaps.

But before either witch can do anything, Prince starts licking the Wicked Witch of the East's ankle.

Toto begins licking the Wicked Witch of the West's ankle.

Dorothy and I glance at each other. What are our dogs doing? Why are they being friendly to the witches? Toto isn't friendly to anyone! And I thought Prince was loyal to me!

But wait . . .

"Ahhhh!" the Wicked Witch of the East cries as her body starts getting weirdly smaller. Is she *shrinking*?

"Nooo!" the Wicked Witch of the West shouts as her body does the same thing.

My eyes widen. Oh my goodness.

The witches are . . . melting!

"The dogs' saliva is making the witches melt!" Frankie cries. "Just like water would!"

OMG. Is anything grosser?

But, yay?

Yay!

The witches get tinier and tinier as they melt down, down, down.

We hear the faintest of shrill cries, and suddenly there is nothing where the witches stood but their capes, hats, brooms, two gray crowns, striped tights, and shoes. The puddles soak right into the ground and disappear.

"Um," Penny says, looking around. "Did Toto and Prince just lick the witches away? With their dog slobber?"

"Yes!" I say disbelievingly. "I think they did!"

Toto and Prince bark proudly, their tails wagging.

"The witches are gone?" Dorothy asks.

"They are!" Frankie cries, her eyes sparkling.

"Hurrah!" Robin says, doing a little dance.

"Good boy!" I tell Prince, scooping him up and nuzzling him close just as Dorothy scoops up Toto and praises him, too.

"The witches are gone!" the Wizard's voice booms out.

A whole bunch of Munchkins and Winkies start running toward us.

They're cheering and clapping.

I spot Orly among the Munchkins, and she sprints over to me and grabs me and Prince in a hug.

"Thank you so much!" she cries. "Because your dogs got rid of the witches — for good — we're no longer under their spell. We're free!"

"We couldn't have escaped in the first place without *you*," I tell Orly, hugging her back.

"It's true," Frankie says with a grin. "Everyone contributed."

The Munchkins and Winkies are all dancing and cheering in celebration.

"Ding-dong, the witches are dead!" Penny starts to sing. Everyone joins in.

Lion does the Floss. Tin Man and Scarecrow do the Macarena.

"The Wizard will reclaim his rule!" the guardian of the gates says. "Hurrah!"

Then Penny stops singing. I look over to her and see that she's running for the spot where the witches melted.

The magic silver shoes are lying there. And so are her checkered sneakers. Yay! Penny snatches them both up and lifts them all above her head, two in each hand, in a V for victory. At last, we can go home!

The gray clouds disappear and blue skies are everywhere. Flowers start to bloom — in all colors of the rainbow. The gray has been lifted.

"But why isn't everything green again?" one of the towns-people asks. "Everything is just regular color. I thought this was the Emerald City."

"Because you're not wearing your glasses," the Wizard says, stepping into the middle of the circle. "I am sorry to tell you this. But I am a fraud. I don't really have any magical powers."

Everyone gasps.

chapter sixteen

Are You a Good Witch or a Bad Witch?

See, I don't deserve to reclaim my rule," the Wizard says, hanging his head. "You all deserve better than me."

There are murmurs through the crowd. They're getting angrier and angrier.

"We should lock him up!"

"Kick him out!"

"Put him in Tigertail Tower!"

"Let the tiger eat him!"

The crowd is slowly closing in on him and us. This isn't good. It's an angry mob! I hold Prince close and look for a way to escape.

Suddenly, a burst of glittery blue appears in front of us.

What's this?

The blue glittery air clears and a woman steps forward. She has gray hair and brown skin and kind eyes. She's wearing a pale blue gown that glistens in the sun like it's made of diamonds. She's also wearing a pale blue pointy hat.

"It's Glinda!" Penny exclaims. "Glinda the Good Witch! Finally! Where has she been?"

"The Munchkins could only call for her now that the Wicked Witch of the East is dead," Frankie explains.

Ah.

Glinda walks over to the two gray crowns and picks them up. The crowns immediately become one. They turn from gray to gold and are encrusted with colorful stones.

Wow!

Swoosh-whoosh. Swoooooop!

I look up. Uh-oh. Winged Monkeys start soaring straight for us.

Oh, noooo! Just when I thought things were improving.

"Hide, everyone!" I cry.

But the Winged Monkeys don't snatch anyone. They land on the ground beside Glinda.

"Don't worry about them," Glinda says. "They have to do the bidding of whoever wears the crown. And right now that's me! Enjoy the Emerald City, monkeys. Have fun!"

The Winged Monkeys cheer. I see one opening up a banana. Two others begin playing what looks like flying tag. Whew.

"The monkeys are kind of cute now," Penny admits.

Glinda looks at the shoes in Penny's hands. "The magic shoes! Aren't they pretty?"

"Yeah," Penny says. "But silver is so last season. Can you change the color?"

"Perhaps," Glinda says, tapping her wand on her chin. "What color were you thinking?"

Oooh. It *would* be cool to see the ruby slippers.

"Red, I guess," Penny says. "Why not, right?"

Glinda waves her magic wand and the magic slippers are now — *poof* — ruby-red shoes. Just like in the movie.

"Yay! Thank you!" Penny picks them up and hands them to me. "Your turn, Abby. You should be the one to take us all home."

Oh! I wasn't expecting that. But I do want to try them on. I step into the shoes. They fit! Of course they do. They're magic shoes. I wave one foot around. I'm wearing the ruby slippers!

I look at Glinda. "So if we all hold hands, I can click my heels together and take us to Kansas?" I ask. My plan is that we'll drop off Dorothy at her home, and then I'll click the heels again to take my friends and me back to Smithville.

Glinda shakes her head. "I'm so sorry, but the shoes can't carry so much weight. One person and maybe a pet — a small one — maximum."

My heart sinks. Crumbs.

"That's it?" Robin asks. "Then how will we all get home?"

"I don't know," I say.

"We can send Dorothy home with the shoes," Frankie says, "but what happens to us?"

"Can the monkeys help?" Penny asks. "They can carry people."

"They can't leave Oz," Frankie says. "It's in the book."

Glinda nods. "That's true." She glances at the Wizard. "Can you help them?" she asks.

"I'm a fraud," the Wizard says sadly. "I don't have magical powers."

"True," Glinda says. "But you did come to Oz in a hot-air balloon. Can't the girls take your hot-air balloon back?"

We all look at one another. Could we?

Frankie shakes her head. "In the book, the Wizard does try to use his hot-air balloon to take Dorothy home, but then Toto jumps out and so does Dorothy. So the Wizard goes away, but we don't know where."

"The hot-air balloon will work this time," Glinda says. "I am confident."

"I'll leave with you," the Wizard says sadly. "These people don't want me here anymore anyway."

"I don't believe that's true," Glinda says. "Everyone!" she calls out to the crowd, and they quiet down. "Listen here! It's true that the Wizard is not really a wizard. But he is a very nice man and an excellent leader. Would you like him to stay and lead the Emerald City, or would you like him to go?"

There are murmurs as all the townspeople gather together to discuss. And then finally we hear, "Stay! He should stay!"

Glinda beams. "The crowd has spoken."

The Wizard is teary. "Thank you!" he tells Glinda. He turns to Tin Man, Scarecrow, and Lion. "Would you all stay with me? And help run Oz?"

"Us? Really?" Lion asks.

"Yes!" the Wizard says. "You're so brave! The way you stormed the Tigertail Tower was inspiring. And Tin Man, you are so kind. The way you comforted Penny when she was scared was really caring. And, Scarecrow, your idea to trick the crowd was very smart. I could use a crew like you to help me run this place!"

Lion blushes, Tin Man smiles, and Scarecrow beams. The three of them look at one another and nod happily.

"We would be honored," Tin Man says.

"And you don't mind if we take your hot-air balloon?" I ask the Wizard.

"Not at all," he says. "Might take me a few hours to set it up and teach you how to use it. Unless any of you know how?"

"Um, no," I say.

"Actually, I do," Robin says. "Kind of. My parents took me to a hot-air balloon festival in Albuquerque last year. It was fun."

"Oh, wow!" I say. Unexpected. "Great."

"But how do we find Smithville?" Frankie asks.

"Go west," the Wizard says. "Follow the sun."

Seems vague, but I guess it will have to do.

"You should go as soon as the sun starts to drop," he adds.

"Okay," I say. "We can't wait much longer than that. We have no idea what time it is back home, so we should get back as soon as possible. But, Dorothy, we understand if you want to go home right now. We know you miss your family."

She links her arms through Robin's and Penny's. "I miss them for sure," she says. "But I'll miss you guys, too. I can wait another hour."

Which means I get more time in the shoes! Woot! Not that I'm using their magic. But still. They're pretty cool.

Penny picks up Toto and in a baby voice says, "I will miss you, Toto, yes I will."

I guess Penny is coming around to dogs after all.

"Shall we have some lunch?" Glinda asks. "I can zap up a feast. Does anyone like pizza?"

My stomach growls. "Everyone likes pizza," I say. "But hold the spiders, frogs, and butterflies."

chapter seventeen

Up, Up, and Away . . .

"Ready?" the Wizard asks.

We all nod.

The hot-air balloon looks awesome. It's huge and multi-colored. Below the balloon is a big basket that we're supposed to stand in. I have no idea how hot-air balloons work, but I'm glad Robin and the Wizard do.

Before we climb into the basket, I take off the ruby slippers and hand them to Dorothy. "Do you know what to do?"

She slips her feet inside the sparkly shoes.

"Just click your heels together three times and tell the shoes where you want to go. They'll take you in three steps," Glinda explains.

"Got it," Dorothy says. Then she pauses. "But . . . are we sold on the plain red?"

Huh?

"Do you want me to change them to something else?" Glinda asks.

Dorothy smiles. "I kind of like the checkered pattern on Penny's shoes. Do you think you could do that?" she asks.

"You have excellent taste," Penny tells Dorothy, who blushes.

Glinda laughs and waves her wand toward the shoes.

They're now checkered red and black. But still glittering.

"Wow. Thank you!" Dorothy says.

"Looking good," I say, and give her a hug. My eyes tear up. "It was great to meet you."

"You too," Dorothy says. "Thank you all for helping me."

I look at Dorothy in her blue-and-white gingham dress,

braids — and checkered red-and-black slippers — with Toto in her arms.

Perfect.

Ruff! Prince barks good-bye to Toto.

Ruff-ruff! Toto barks back. He leaps out of Dorothy's arms and runs right over to Prince. But they don't fight. Instead, Prince leans against Toto. Aw, is Prince giving Toto a hug? I think they are sad to say good-bye. They've come so far together — from not getting along, to working together to save us all!

Dorothy scoops up Toto again and closes her eyes. She clicks her heels together three times. "Take me home," she says. "Take me home. Take me home."

Poof!

And she's gone.

Glinda closes her eyes and opens them three seconds later. "Dorothy and Toto are already home! I saw her safely land and run into her aunt's and uncle's arms."

Whew.

"Ready?" Bob the Wizard asks, sweeping his arm toward the hot-air balloon.

"Ready!" I say as Frankie, Robin, Penny, and I — carrying Prince — get in the basket of the balloon. I sneeze. I really am ready to get home and into bed.

"You're good, Robin?" Bob asks. He gave her a brief review before to make sure she knew what to do.

"Great," Robin says. "The hot-air makes you go higher. And cool air makes you go lower."

"Exactly," the Wizard says.

I wave down at the crowd as the balloon starts to rise.

Glinda, Scarecrow, Tin Man, and Lion are all waving and smiling.

I wave at the Munchkins and the Winkies.

And then suddenly we're flying up, up, and away. It's not scary like when the flying monkeys captured us, or when the tornado lifted Robin's tree house. It feels peaceful and easy, like we're floating on a cloud.

We sail over the Emerald City and I see the yellow brick road below us.

I look out on Oz and smile. This has been an amazing adventure!

But then I freeze.

Because standing right there on the yellow brick road . . .

Is GLUCK.

He's not in disguise: He looks like himself — white-blond choppy hair, ice-blue eyes. And I can see the black wings on his back!

No!

"Robin, can you go any higher or faster?!" I cry. "I see Gluck!"

"What's that in Gluck's hand?" Frankie asks, straining to see.

We all look.

"It's a bow and arrow," I say.

"What is he doing with a . . ." Robin asks, but her voice trails off as we see what he's up to. He pulls the bow back and the arrow comes flying right toward us.

Nooooo!!!

"Good-bye, suckers!" Gluck shouts into the sky.

We all scream and duck down into the basket.

But the arrow goes right into the balloon, tearing a hole right through it.

"Oh, no!" Frankie cries.

The balloon suddenly starts to zigzag in the sky. We all hold on for dear life.

"This is bad," Robin says. "Really, really bad."

The balloon starts to drop. And tilt. Suddenly, we're floating *down* instead of up. We're descending faster. And faster.

"Guys, hold on to the side!" I scream. "We're going to crash into that field of red flowers!"

chapter eighteen

Sleepy Time

t *hud.*

Thankfully, the soft red flowers provide a cushion, so the landing isn't that hard. We stand up in the hot-air balloon, relieved to be okay.

But wait. No! The red flowers are the poppies! The ones that made the others fall asleep last time. Are you kidding me? "Nobody breathe!" I cry. "Everyone, hold your noses!"

"It's too late," Frankie says, beginning to swoon. "I'm

tired again." She sits down, then lies down. In seconds she's asleep. Ahhhh!

"Robin, do not breathe in, do you hear me, we need you, do not breath —"

But Robin's curled up on the floor of the basket, snoring, too.

"Noooo," I say.

Prince is also curled up and snoring.

"Why am I still awake?" Penny asks. She sneezes.

I look at her. I half smile. "You caught my cold?"

She laughs. "I did. I actually did. I never thought I'd be so happy to get a cold."

"Seriously," I say, sneezing, too. "Now, how do we get out of here?"

She looks up at the tear in the balloon. "We need to plug the hole."

"But with what?" I ask.

"Oh!" Penny exclaims. "Look what I have! My last piece! I saved it!" She takes the grape bubble gum out of her pocket and chews it for a few seconds. "Mmm. The flavor is so good at the beginning, right?"

Then she carefully climbs up the edge of the basket to find the hole. "I think this works," she says, taking the gum out of her mouth and spreading it out to close up the hole. It's kind of gross, but who cares?

"Great," I say. "Now we only have to figure out how to fly this thing."

"I saw Robin do this," Penny says, pressing a button.

"And I saw her do *this*," I say, pulling a lever.

The basket starts to shake a bit and slowly rise back off the ground.

"We did it!" Penny says.

"The hot-air makes you go higher," I say, remembering. "And cool air makes you go lower. Right? I think that's what Robin said."

Penny nods.

Hot-air, higher. Cool air, lower. Got it — I think!

"So we just have to make the heat hotter or cooler

depending on how the breeze is carrying us," Penny says, rushing over to the knob controls. One says HOT and one says COLD.

"It's working!" I cry. "And now we just head west?"

"That's what he said."

"Okay, then," I say. "That's what we'll do."

"Abby —" Penny says.

"Yeah?"

She smiles at me. "This was fun. I'm glad I got to come with you into a story again."

"It was. And I'm glad you were here with me," I admit.

"Whoa. What's that?" Penny asks.

In front of us is a pale, swirling blue mist.

"It's something magical," I say, thinking of the swirling purple portal that always takes me home from fairy tales. "Go into it!"

As soon as we float into the mist, the balloon starts spinning really fast, like a Tilt-A-Whirl.

I squeeze my eyes shut. I have no idea what's about to happen!

The balloon spins and twirls and goes sideways. I hold on to the still-sleeping Robin and Frankie and Prince so they don't fly out. We go sliding to the left. Then to the right as the balloon straightens. Suddenly, we're just floating. I can't see a thing.

CLUNK!

The next thing I know, the basket lands on something hard.

I open my eyes. The pale blue mist disappears from outside the window.

We're back in the tree house. Robin, Frankie, and Prince are still asleep.

What happened? How is the tree house in one piece? Did Glinda do that? She must have.

"Look!" Penny cries, her eyes wide. But in awe, not fear.

"What?" I ask, turning to where she's pointing out the window.

It's a rainbow! So many colors stretch from one side of the backyard to the other in a huge arc.

"Like the song!" she says. "Remember the song? 'Somewhere, over the rainbow'!"

"I remember," I say, giggling.

Frankie and Robin start to stir.

Frankie sits up and adjusts her glasses. "Wow, did I fall asleep?"

"Yup," I say. "Because of the poppies."

"Abby gave me her cold so I didn't," Penny says.

"You're welcome," I say with a laugh.

"Poppies?" Frankie asks. "What poppies? Did we pick a new topic for the project? Are we giving out flowers or something?"

Robin stretches her arms over her head in a yawn. "Why do I taste pizza in my mouth?"

"You don't remember?" Penny asks, looking from Frankie to Robin.

"Remember what?" Robin asks.

Penny and I look at each other. The poppy sleep took away Frankie's and Robin's memories of the entire trip to Oz! They clearly don't remember anything. Again! I wonder why the poppies didn't erase their memories the first time they fell asleep?

Penny leans closer to them. *"The Wiz —"*

"The whisper. You don't remember what I whispered?" I interrupt.

I give Penny a meaningful look. It's best if we continue to keep the secret between the two of us. For now.

"The whisper?" Robin asks. "Huh?"

"Look at that amazing rainbow," I say, trying to distract them.

"So pretty!" Frankie says. She and Robin go over to the window to look out.

Prince rolls over and opens one eye.

"Good morning," I say to him, scratching behind his ear. I wonder if he remembers his new friend Toto or not. I hope he does.

"Hi, Prince," Penny says, kneeling down in front of him and petting his fur. "What a sweetie."

"A sweetie?" Robin asks, turning around. "Since when? You hated dogs ten minutes ago!"

"What?" Penny says, scrunching up her face as if what Robin just said made no sense. "I did not!"

"You said dogs slobber and smell," Frankie reminds her.

"They do," Penny says. "Sometimes. But Toto —"

"Toto?" Frankie asks, raising an eyebrow.

"Not all dogs are bad," she finishes. "Long story."

She smiles at me. I smile at her.

"Can we go outside and look at the rainbow?" Robin asks. "It's so pretty."

"We should finish up and choose our project idea first," Frankie says. "I forget where we were."

"I think you each suggested something," Robin says, frowning. "I didn't have any good ideas. And then you were arguing about it."

"Right," I say, wincing. Arguing wasn't getting us

anywhere, that's for sure. "Why don't we each say our idea again and then take a vote? That seems the fairest way."

Penny nods. "Mine was that we give style advice. But you guys thought that might be too mean."

"You *are* good with fashion," I say. "I do really like the pattern on your shoes."

She smiles. "Thanks."

"Mine was that we offer a dog-walking service," I say. "But Penny pointed out that not everyone has a dog."

"That's true," Penny says, giving Prince another stroke. "Although walking dogs might be kind of fun."

"My idea was a tutoring service," Frankie says.

Robin nodded. "But I said that I can't teach anything." She sighs. "I didn't have an idea, either. Sorry I'm so brainless at this stuff!"

"You have an amazing brain," I tell her. "Now let's vote. All in favor of the tutoring company?"

Penny and I both raise our hands.

Frankie looks surprised. "But . . ."

"Your idea is my favorite," I tell her, and Penny agrees.

"A tutoring company is a great idea," Penny explains. "And everyone is good at something. I can give art lessons. Abby can teach people about books. You, Frankie, can teach science and math. And Robin can teach hot-air ballooning!"

"Huh?" Frankie asks.

Robin looks at Penny quizzically. "How did you know I can steer a hot-air balloon?"

Penny's eyes widen. "Oh, um. Isn't there a picture of you doing it in your house?"

Whew. Good thinking, Penny!

Robin considers this. "Oh, right. Yeah. Okay. But how many people need to learn hot-air ballooning?"

"You never know when it will come in handy," I say cheerfully. "Plus, don't forget you're also a really good swimmer."

"Thanks," Robin says. "I am also good at bike riding. And spelling, actually."

"See? There's a lot you can teach people," I tell Robin. "I bet you'll be a great teacher."

Robin beams.

"So we're choosing my idea?" Frankie asks.

"Works for me," Robin says, and Penny and I nod.

Frankie's shoulders melt. "It means a lot to me. I . . ." Her voice catches. "I know I was being kind of cranky before. But it's because . . . well . . . my dad has to be away for six months for his job. And I've been really bummed."

"Oh, Frankie," I say, trying to sound surprised. I put my arm around her. "We're here whenever you want to talk."

"Yes," Penny says. "We love you. FRAP forever!"

"FRAP forever," Robin echoes. "Now let's go outside and look at that rainbow. Maybe we'll find a pot of gold."

I smile. "Or a yellow brick road."

chapter nineteen

There's No Place Like Home

I give a little tap on the mirror in my basement. "Maryrose?" I call. "Maryrose, are you there?"

Please answer! Sometimes she doesn't. But I have to tell her what happened.

When I came home and my mom saw how sick I looked, she told me to get right into bed, and that she would bring me a bowl of chicken soup. But I need to talk to Maryrose first!

The glass part of the mirror turns purple and starts swirling. Yay!

Achoo! I sneeze.

A woman's face and hair is silhouetted in the mirror.

"Bless you!" Maryrose says.

"Thanks," I say, sniffling.

"That was some adventure, huh?" Maryrose says.

I nod. "Gluck tried to trap me again! He *really* doesn't want me helping you."

"I know," she says. "But you escaped! Good job! Without any help from me!"

"Wait. That blue cloud wasn't you?"

"No," she says. "That was Glinda. She's wonderful, though. I knew her a long time ago . . . before I was trapped. She also added in a little memory-erasing dust in the poppies. Sorry Penny got your cold."

"It's okay," I say. "And Maryrose — I'll save you. One day, I promise."

"Thank you," Maryrose says.

"Abby!" Jonah calls from the landing. "Mom wants you to get into bed!"

I turn my head toward the stairs. "Coming!" I call up. I look back at the mirror but Maryrose is already misting away.

"What were you doing?" Jonah asks, running down the stairs.

I lower my voice. "I was talking with Maryrose."

Jonah's eyes widen. "About what? Did you go somewhere without me?"

"Kind of . . ." Quickly, in a whisper, I launch into the whole story.

His eyes widen even more as I tell him about the tree house, the witches, the dungeon, the Scarecrow, the Tin Man, the Lion, the tiger, and dogs, and of course, the flying monkeys.

"The flying monkeys carried you?" Jonah cries. "No fair! I wish I could've been there."

"Sorry," I say. "It was really scary, though."

"I love scary! How come Gluck never tries to trap me anywhere? Huh? Isn't he worried about *me*? Maybe he wants to take me into *Star Wars* or something?"

"Next time I see him I'll ask," I say with a laugh.

"You're lucky you and your friends made it home," Jonah says.

"I know," I say.

I'm lucky my friends and I were able to work together to *get* us home.

Later, I'm settled in my bed, propped up on my pillows with a folding table in front of me.

"Thanks, Mom," I say as she sets down a bowl of steaming chicken soup. Mmm.

She kisses my forehead. "Feel better, sweetie. Here's the book you left downstairs this morning." She puts a copy of *The Wonderful Wizard of Oz* on my bed.

"I left this book downstairs?" I ask.

"Didn't you?" my mom asks, frowning. "I saw it in the kitchen and figured it was yours."

"I . . ." I didn't have a copy of *The Wonderful Wizard of Oz* this morning! But I'm happy to have it now. But where did it come from? Maryrose? Glinda? Either way, I'm excited to finally read it.

When my mom leaves, I start eating my chicken soup while opening the book.

OMG. No, OM*W*!

We're in it! In the book! There are full-on illustrations of my friends and me in the book! There I am, holding Prince, and there are Frankie and Robin and Penny.

At first we're all standing separately, looking annoyed at each other. Only toward the end do we start working together.

On the last page is a big illustration of all of us with our arms around one another — me (holding Prince), Penny, Frankie, Robin, Scarecrow, Tin Man, Lion, Bob the Wizard, and of course Dorothy, in her blue-and-white dress. Her brown hair is in braids, Toto is in in her lap. And she's wearing . . .

I lean closer to see.

The red-and-black sparkly shoes.

Hah. Penny would approve.

I lean back against my pillows and swallow another spoonful of Mom's chicken soup.

Mmmm. I'm feeling better already. There really is no place like home.

I glance back at the book. And there's nothing like good stories. Or good friends.

Turn the page for some magical *fun* and games!

A Note From the Author

Dear Reader,

I am so excited to share the second Whatever After Special Edition with you!

After tossing Abby into so many different fairy tales — and, in the first Special Edition, into *Alice's Adventures in Wonderland* — I finally have her visiting my favorite magical story of them all . . . *The Wonderful Wizard of Oz*!

As a kid, I must have watched the movie *The Wizard of Oz* at least a hundred times — not exaggerating. I watched it over and over again, and then a few more times for good luck. The story was so much fun. I, too, wanted to follow a yellow brick road to a magical emerald city. I wanted a feisty dog named Toto, and loyal travel companions like the Scarecrow, the Tin Man, and the Lion. I also really, really wanted ruby slippers — I once even got grounded for coloring in my brand-spankin'-new white sneakers with a red marker. Oops!

But no matter how many times I wished for magical ruby

slippers of my own, they never appeared on my feet, or in my closet. And of course, even if they had appeared, I knew I wouldn't *actually* get to travel to the Land of Oz.

Now, as a grown-up, I still don't have ruby slippers of my own (I've searched on Zappos). I don't have a feisty dog (yet). But I do have a wonderful family and loyal friends. And best of all, I was finally able to make my dream of visiting Oz come true. How? By writing this book! I got to skip down the yellow brick road, meet all the awesome characters of Oz, explore the Emerald City, and click my heels together three times. And you know what's even more amazing? I get to take you all there with me.

There's no place like home, there's no place like Oz, and there's no place like a favorite book.

Happy reading!

XO

Sarah Mlynowski

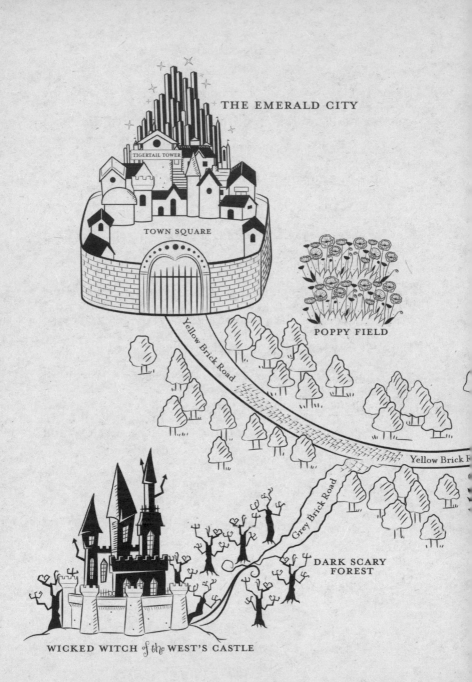

ABBY'S
MAP of OZ

MUNCHKINLAND

LANDING
AREA

Yellow Brick Road

Grey Brick Road

CORNFIELDS

WICKED WITCH of the EAST'S CASTLE

Write Your Own Story

One day, you're relaxing in your room, rereading your favorite book, when suddenly the page starts swirling and sucks you inside. AHHHH! What and who do you see?

You're not going to mess the story up. You're not going to mess the story up. You're not going to . . . OOPS. You messed the story up. How did you mess the story up?

You've got to fix the ending! Or maybe you don't?! What do you do?

It's pizza night at home (hold the spider toppings) and you do NOT want to miss it. How do you get home? And how does the story end now?

Crossword Puzzle

Test your Whatever After knowledge with this crossword puzzle!*

* Answer key on page 222

DOWN

1. The fairy who's trapped in Abby and Jonah's magic mirror

3. Job that Abby and Jonah's parents both have

4. Where the magic mirror is in Abby and Jonah's house

5. The number of times Abby and Jonah have to knock on the magic mirror to get slurped into a fairy tale

7. Abby's friend whose name is a type of bird

9. Something Jonah really, really likes to eat

ACROSS

2. The town where Abby and Jonah live

6. Author _____ Mlynowski

8. Abby's friend who wears glasses

10. Animals Penny loves (before she likes dogs)

Word Search

Find these twelve words (they can be found diagonally, across, up, and down!)*

Tigertail, Dotty, Emerald City, Penny, Glinda, tree house, hot air balloon, poppies, Winkies, Munchkins, yellow brick road, silver slippers

```
D Y T T O D G J P N R S L M S
U A N B Y T M Z O W M R E Q X
U A O N C X A Z A S C E M U B
I E Z R E Y K C Y Y Z P P W F
L E Y W K P F R S L G P L Y W
E M M U N C H K I N S I G J I
S E H O T A I R B A L L O O N
U R W T Z P T R O N I S G H K
O A X R M A O U B N D R Z Y I
H L W N K I I P D W Q E N T E
E D B P L Y T A P W O V Z N S
E C L I A T R E G I T L L U J
R I A J J A F V D R E I L U P
T T H X E K H S L R M S J E Y
M Y C P H Z J Y F T A L N Q Y
```

212

Fill in the Blanks

Fill in the Blanks #1

Fill in this list with each type of word to create your own stories:

a. Name _____

b. A type of food (singluar) _____

c. Number _____

d. Type of food (plural) _____

e. Number _____

f. Place _____

g. Job (plural) _____

h. Item of clothing (plural) _____

i. Number _____

j. Noun _____

k. Noun _____

l. Type of room _____

m. Adjective _____

n. Noun _____

o. Place _____

p. Place --

q. Place --

✳ From *Whatever After Book 2: If the Shoe Fits*

Too Much (d) _____ !

"Hello? Maryrose? Are you there?" I know I said Maryrose lives inside the mirror, but truthfully, I'm not sure. All I know is that Maryrose has something to do with the mirror. I think. I really don't know much. I sigh. "Maybe we imagined the whole thing."

"No way," Jonah says. "We were there. I know we were. We met (a) _____! We ate her (b) _____ sandwiches! Yum. I wish Mom and Dad would make them one night for dinner."

I snort. First of all, (a) _____'s (b) _____ sandwiches were gross. And second, the likelihood of Mom and Dad trying a new recipe these days is very unlikely. Like (e) _____ in a bajillion. They haven't cooked in weeks. We've ordered (d) _____ for the last two — no, make that (e) _____ — nights in a row.

Don't get me wrong, I like (d) _____. What ten-year-old doesn't like (d) _____? What adult doesn't like (d) _____? Jonah LOVES (d) _____, even though he insists on dipping the crust in ketchup, which is totally gross. But (e) _____ nights in a row is extreme.

What happened to cooking? What happened to meat loaf? What happened to salad?

My parents used to cook all the time, before we moved to (f) _____. They had time to cook then. Now they work all the time. They're (g) _____ and just started their own firm. I keep telling them I'm old enough to do the cooking, but they won't listen. Just because I nearly burned down our old house when I put my (h) _____ in the toaster (i) _____ time(s). What can I say? I wanted toasty (h) _____. They won't even let me near the (j) _____, which makes no sense. Fine. I used too much (k) _____ and turned the (l) _____ into a (m) _____ (n) _____, but also, only (i) _____ time(s).

I yawn. "Let's go back to bed."

"But I want an adventure! Maybe the mirror can take us to other places, too. Like (o) _____! Or (p) _____! Or (q)_____!"

Fill in the Blanks #2

a. Verb ending in –ing ---------------------------------

b. Adjective ---------------------------------

c. Adjective ---------------------------------

d. Noun (plural) ---------------------------------

e. Title of a story ---------------------------------

f. Verb ending in –ing ---------------------------------

g. Animal ---------------------------------

h. Adjective ---------------------------------

i. Adjective ending in –er ---------------------------------

j. Item of clothing (plural) ---------------------------------

k. Noun ---------------------------------

l. Adjective ---------------------------------

m. Adjective ---------------------------------

n. Verb ending in –ing ---------------------------------

o. Job title ---------------------------------

p. Location ---------------------------------

q. Noun ---------------------------------

*From *Whatever After Book 8: Once Upon a Frog*

The (o) _____ is Coming!

I see Jonah's head (a) _____ left, then right. "It looks like a
(p) _____," he says. "But with really (b) _____ trees. Really
(b) _____ ones. (e) _____ ones. They could even be (d) _____!
Are you sure we're not in (e) _____?"

"Jonah, we are NOT in (e) _____! I am stuck in a well with a
(f) _____ (g) _____!"

"Fine," Jonah huffs. "It's really (h) _____ up here," he adds.
"You might want to stay down there, know-it-all. Bet it's
(i) _____."

My flannel (j) _____ are sticking to me. Not exactly comfortable. "I think I'd rather get out of the bottom of the well, thanks.
Is there a (k) _____ out there?"

"No (k) _____," he says. "Not much of anything."

I turn to Frederic. "Any ideas?"

"Can you climb up?" the (g) _____ suggests.

I feel the inside of the well to see if there are ridges or anything
to dig my feet into, but it feels (l) _____. "Let me try," I say, and
attempt to pull myself up. I can't. "I guess you wouldn't be able
to give me a boost," I say to Frederic.

"My push-ups have made me (m) _____," he reminds me. "But
not that (m) _____."

Ruff! Ruff, ruff! Ruff! I hear from above. *Ruff! Ruff, ruff! Ruff!*

Prince is (n) _____ the way he does when the doorbell rings.

"What's wrong?" I call up to Jonah.

"Someone's coming!" Jonah says.

"It's probably the (o) _____!" I cry. Crumbs. I was hoping to get out of here first. Now what? I have to hide. So do Prince and Jonah! "Go hide!" I tell my brother.

"Where?"

"You said you're in a (p) _____. Go find a (q) _____! Quick, so she doesn't see you!" I say. "We want the story to continue the way it's supposed to!"

Although what Jonah said before was right. We always mess up the stories.

"Whatever you say, Abby!" Jonah calls back. He ducks out of sight.

"Is she coming now?" Frederic asks. His bulging eyes look up, then back at me.

I nod. I listen for footsteps or voices but don't hear anything. The (o) _____ has to stop at the well. I take a deep breath. She will. It's part of the original story.

Fill in the Blanks #3

a. Food _____

b. Job title _____

c. Type of party _____

d. Noun (plural) _____

e. Body part _____

f. Noun (plural) _____

g. Food (plural) _____

h. Animal _____

i. Adjective _____

j. Adjective _____

k. Adjective _____

l. Noun (plural) _____

* From *Whatever After Book 12: Seeing Red*

Nana's Here!

"Nana, please tell me I can go to Penny's?" I beg.

Please say yes. Pleeeeeeeeeaze!

"I'm sorry, Abby, but no," Nana tells me, dipping a slice of (a) _____ into the egg mixture she's whipped up.

"You don't even like Penny," Jonah reminds me.

I frown at Jonah. "I like her sometimes!" I say to him. Then I look back at my nana. Maybe I can talk her into it. I just have to lay out the facts. My parents are lawyers, and that's how they win their trials. By pleading their cases. When I grow up, I want to be a lawyer, too — well, I want to be a (b) _____, but you have to be a lawyer first — so this will be good practice.

"It's a(n) (c) _____," I explain to Nana, "and my two best (d) _____ will be there. I don't want to be left out."

Nana shakes her (e) _____. "I came to spend time with you, Abby. So the answer is no. Maybe you can sleep over next weekend."

Penny isn't having a(n) (c) _____ NEXT weekend. She's having a(n) (c) _____ THIS weekend. She's having a(n) (c) _____ TONIGHT.

"But I'm going to miss all the stuff," I say. "They're going to stay up late telling (f) _____ and I won't know anything!"

"We can stay up late telling (f) _____," Nana says.

Nanas are for hugs and bedtime stories. Not for (f) _____.

"I'll get out the (g) _____," Jonah offers.

"Thank you, sweetheart," Nana says to him.

"So I really can't go?" I ask Nana with my best (h) _____ eyes. That means they get very (i) _____ and (j) _____ and match the (k) _____ smile on my face.

"No," she says. There's a slight DO NOT ASK ME AGAIN edge to her tone.

(l) _____.

Crossword Puzzle Answer Key*

DOWN

1. Maryrose

3. lawyer

4. basement

5. three

7. Robin

9. ketchup

ACROSS

2. Smithville

6. Sarah

8. Frankie

10. horses

*From the Crossword Puzzle on page 210

Word Search Answer Key*

```
D Y T T O D G J P N R S L M S
U A N B Y T M Z O W M R E Q X
U A O N C X A Z A S C E M U B
I E Z R E Y K C Y Y Z P P W F
L E Y W K P F R S L G P L Y W
E M U N C H K I N S I G J I
S E H O T A I R B A L L O O N
U R W T Z P T R O N I S G H K
O A X R M A O U B N D R Z Y I
H L W N K I I P D W Q E N T E
E D B P L Y T A P W O V Z N S
E C L I A T R E G I T L L U J
R I A J J A F V D R E I L U P
T T H X E K H S L R M S J E Y
M Y C P H Z J Y F T A L N Q Y
```

* From the Word Search on page 212

Don't miss Abby and Jonah's next adventure,
where they fall into the tale of *Goldilocks and the Three Bears*!

Look for:

Whatever After #14: GOOD AS GOLD

acknowledgments

Magical thank-yous to:

Everyone at Scholastic: Aimee Friedman, Taylan Salvati, Charisse Meloto, Lauren Donovan, Rachel Feld, Erin Berger, Olivia Valcarce, Melissa Schirmer, Elizabeth Parisi, Abby McAden, David Levithan, Lizette Serrano, Emily Heddleson, Robin Hoffman, Sue Flynn, and everyone in Sales and in the School Channels.

My amazing agents, Laura Dail and Samantha Fabien, Austin Denesuk, Matthew Snyder, and Berni Barta, and queen of publicity, Deb Shapiro. Rachel and Terry Winter! For everything!

Lauren Walters and Caitlen Patton who did all the stuff.

All my friends, family, writing buddies, and first readers: Targia Alphonse, Tara Altebrando, Bonnie Altro, Elissa Ambrose, Robert Ambrose, Jennifer Barnes, the Bilermans, Julie Buxbaum, Jess Braun, Max Brallier, Rose Brock, Jeremy Cammy, the Dalven-Swidlers, Julia DeVillers, Elizabeth Eulberg, Leslie Margolis, the Finkelstein-Mitchells, Stuart Gibbs, Karina Van Glaser, Alan Gratz, the Greens,

DON'T MISS ABBY AND JONAH'S NEXT ADVENTURE!

Whatever After #14

GOOD AS GOLD

In the story of *Goldilocks and the Three Bears*, there's porridge to sample and beds to test out! But if Abby and Jonah help Goldilocks, will they run into trouble with the Bear family?

Read all the **Whatever After** books!

Whatever After #1: FAIREST of ALL

In their first adventure, Abby and Jonah wind up in the story of Snow White. But when they stop Snow from eating the poisoned apple, they realize they've messed up the whole story! Can they fix it — and still find Snow her happy ending?

Whatever After #2: IF the SHOE FITS

This time, Abby and Jonah find themselves in Cinderella's story. When Cinderella breaks her foot, the glass slipper won't fit! With a little bit of magic, quick thinking, and luck, can Abby and her brother save the day?

Whatever After #3: SINK or SWIM

Abby and Jonah are pulled into the tale of *The Little Mermaid* — a story with an ending that is *not* happy. So Abby and Jonah mess it up on purpose! Can they convince the mermaid to keep her tail before it's too late?

Whatever After #4: DREAM ON

Abby and Jonah are lost in Sleeping Beauty's story, along with Abby's friend Robin. Before they know it, Sleeping Beauty is wide awake and Robin is fast asleep. How will Abby and Jonah make things right?

Whatever After #5: BAD HAIR DAY

When Abby and Jonah fall into Rapunzel's story, they mess everything up by giving Rapunzel a haircut! Can they untangle this fairy tale disaster in time?

Whatever After #6: COLD AS ICE

When their dog, Prince, runs through the mirror, Abby and Jonah have no choice but to follow him into the story of the Snow Queen. It's a winter wonderland . . . but the Snow Queen is mean, and she FREEZES Prince! Can Abby and Jonah save their dog . . . and themselves?

Whatever After #7: BEAUTY QUEEN

Abby and Jonah fall into the story of *Beauty and the Beast*. When Jonah is the one taken prisoner instead of Beauty, Abby has to find a way to fix this fairy tale . . . before things get pretty ugly!

Whatever After #8: ONCE upon a FROG

When Abby and Jonah fall into the story of *The Frog Prince*, they realize the princess is so rude they don't even *want* her help! But will they be able to figure out how to turn the frog back into a prince all by themselves?

Whatever After #9: GENIE in a BOTTLE

The mirror has dropped Abby and Jonah into the story of *Aladdin*! But when things go wrong with the genie, the siblings have to escape an enchanted cave, learn to fly a magic carpet, and figure out WHAT to wish for . . . so they can help Aladdin and get back home!

Whatever After #10: SUGAR and SPICE

When Abby and Jonah fall into *Hansel and Gretel*, they can't wait to see the witch's cake house (yum). But they didn't count on the witch trapping them there! Can they escape and make it back to home sweet home?

Whatever After #11: TWO PEAS in a POD

When Abby lands in *The Princess and the Pea*—and has trouble falling asleep on a giant stack of mattresses—everyone in the kingdom thinks SHE is the princess they've all been waiting for. Though Abby loves the royal treatment, she and Jonah need to find a real princess to rule the kingdom . . . and get back home in time!

Whatever After #12: SEEING RED

My, what big trouble we're in! When Abby and Jonah fall into *Little Red Riding Hood*, they're determined to save Little Red and her grandma from being eaten by the big, bad wolf. But there's quite a surprise in store when the siblings arrive at Little Red's grandma's house.

Whatever After #13: SPILL the BEANS

Abby and Jonah FINALLY land in the story of *Jack and the Beanstalk*! But when they end up with the magic beans, can they get Jack out of his gigantic troubles?

Whatever After #14: GOOD as GOLD

In the story of *Goldilocks and the Three Bears*, there's porridge to sample and beds to test out! But if Abby and Jonah help Goldilocks, will they run into trouble with the Bear family?

Whatever After Special Edition #1: ABBY in WONDERLAND

In this Special Edition, Abby and three of her friends fall down a rabbit hole into *Alice's Adventures in Wonderland*! They meet the Mad Hatter, the caterpillar, and Alice herself . . . but only solving a riddle from the Cheshire Cat can help them escape the terrible Queen of Hearts. Includes magical games and an interview with the author!

Redefine
"Happily Ever After"

Read the bestselling series by Sarah Mlynowski!

"Hilarious...with unexpected plot twists and plenty of girl power."—*Booklist*

📖SCHOLASTIC
scholastic.com/whateverafter

WHATEVERAFTER14

WHAT HAPPENS WHEN YOUR MAGIC GOES UPSIDE-DOWN?

From bestselling authors SARAH MLYNOWSKI, LAUREN MYRACLE, and EMILY JENKINS comes a series about finding your own kind of magic.